AnneMar~~ ~

Copyright 2018 E~

Text Copyright (c) 2018 AnneMarie Brear
First published 2012 as Woodland Daughter by
AnneMarie Brear
All Rights Reserved
ISBN 978-1-9998650-2-3

1

Eden's Conflict

Published novels:

Eden's Conflict

ANNEMARIE BREAR

Chapter 1

North Yorkshire, England.
August 1901

Eden lay on the cushioning grass with her eyes closed against the brightness, enjoying the sunshine on her face. Insects buzzed by her head, sounding as lazy as she felt. The summer day's warmth bathed her body through the thin linen dress of blue. Her limbs weighed heavy; her mind sluggish.

Squeals of laughter carried on the hot breeze. Her daughters splashed in the River Aire where it tumbled over the rocks in a noisy riot. The girls were likely trying to drench their father as best they could.

She wiggled a little on her spongy bed, squashing the grass and releasing its scent. A sigh of complete contentment left her, and she smiled with guilty pleasure. Idle days like these were rare and most precious. All in her world was good.

'How do I awaken such a sleeping beauty?'

Eden opened one eye and spied her husband, who stood a few feet away with a mischievous expression on his face. 'Not with wet hands, I can tell you that now, Nathan Harris!'

He flopped down on his side and laid his head on her chest. 'You're a cruel woman, wife.'

'Indeed.' She closed her eyes again and stroked his dark brown hair. 'Are the girls dreadfully wet?'

4

'Aye and happy with it.' He nuzzled her breast, his hand straying down her skirts. 'In fact, they're so busy larking about we can have a minute or two of fun-'

'You think so, hey?' Chuckling, she grasped his wandering hand. 'I'd much prefer to just lie here quietly and do nothing for a change.'

'Well you lie quiet and *I'll* have some fun...' His voice dropped to a husky whisper and he nibbled the soft skin below her left ear.

Eden wrapped her arms around his neck, curling her fingers into his hair. 'I adore you, husband.'

'Aww, my girl...' Nathan kissed her and then hitched himself up onto his elbow, his love for her shining in his light grey eyes.

She caressed his cheek, rough with bristles. 'I'm a couple of years from thirty, hardly a girl any longer.'

'You'll always be my girl to love.' He blocked out the sun as he lowered his head for another soft tender kiss that tasted of the light ale he'd drunk earlier when they ate. Rubbing his nose on hers, his hands spanned her waist as he pulled her tightly against him. 'Even when you're old and grey and with no teeth, you'll still be my girl.'

Spluttering with laughter, she slapped him away. 'You cheeky beggar! Call yourself a lover?'

Nathan rolled onto his back, bringing her with him. 'Do you want me to show you how much of a lover I can be?' He undid the top button of her dress but at that moment their daughters, Josephine and Lillie came running up the bank.

Sitting up and straightening her skirt, Eden smiled at her darling girls, who fell in a tangle of wet petticoats and giggles. Unlike many other children of the area, her daughters were healthy and well fed. They hadn't been put to work in the numerous mills or coal mines littering the district and instead attended the local village school. She and Nathan both agreed that their daughters would be educated, like their parents, to give them better advantages in their lives.

Listening to Josephine tell Nathan about the colours of a dragonfly she saw, Eden handed out red apples, plucked from their own orchard trees. After the girls had run off again, Eden packed up their small picnic.

'Where did the time go, Eden? When did they stop being babies?' Nathan murmured watching them run along the bank squealing with innocent joy.

She looked up at him. 'They are only seven and six, not adults yet.'

'Aye, I know, but I liked it best when they fell asleep in my arms. I felt I could protect them better then.'

'You can protect them now.'

'Not like I want to. Sometimes I want to shut the cottage door and never open it again.'

She sat back on her heels and studied him. Not for the first time did she notice the fine sprinkle of silver in his dark hair, that the lines running from his nose to mouth were deeper. He was a good-looking man, a quiet man. What they called a deep thinker in these parts. He pondered and weighed up his thoughts and actions, which was in contrast to her. She did everything in a hurry, always eager to start the next task or talk about another subject. She thrived on being busy and that's why today was so unique. For the first time in a long while she had actually sat and done nothing, except eat and watch her family. Now, Nathan's turn of mood had dimmed her glow of happiness. As much as she loved him, sometimes it was hard living with such a serious man.

He turned to her; his smile sad. 'Take no notice of me. You know what I'm like.' He jumped to his feet. 'I'll go find the girls.'

Eden stood and reached out to take his hand, halting him. 'We've had a wonderful day together.'

'Aye.'

She stepped closer and kissed him. 'And now I no longer work at the Hall, we can have many more days like this.'

He let out a long sigh and traced her jaw line with his finger. 'I'm a happier man knowing your time there is done. Annabella should have released you years ago and let you be with your family. She didn't really need you or could have replaced you.'

'I didn't want to be released, I enjoyed being her companion. We are very close. She is like a sister.'

'But she's married now and needs you no more.'

She moved away from him. 'That's cruel. You make me feel guilty for keeping my links with the Bradburys.'

'I'm sorry, but that family has too strong a hold over you.' He glanced away. 'They always have done.'

'We've been together since we were children. Why must you bring this up again? You know how much I love Annabella. You know the ties between our two families.'

'Aye I do. I've been the one who suffered because of it.'

She stared at him, amazed at the bitterness of his words. 'That's not fair, Nathan. We live a good life because of the friendship we hold with the Bradburys.'

He grunted. 'You may have a friendship. I simply work for them.'

'They think highly of you.'

'As long as I do my job right and earn them money. It's not as if we dine with them or are invited to their house for high tea.'

'I have dined with them informally,' she argued, her anger building. 'I may not be their social equal, but they have never made me feel-'

'I don't want to row with you, not today. Besides, we need never have this argument again now you're home for good.' After a quick kiss on the nose, he left her to consider his remark.

Frustrated by the quarrel, she folded the old blanket they had used as a table and tried not to condemn his feelings. However, the Hall and the people in it played an enormous part in her life and had done long before she met Nathan. For ten years she had been companion to Annabella, the daughter of Colonel James Bradbury, but even before that official role she was childhood playmate to Annabella and her older brothers, Joel and Charlie. She always made up one of their party as they roamed the woods, frolicked in the river, went shooting and on picnics. She felt the family was an extension to her own, though there were times when it was difficult to be in a position of somewhere between servant and friend. Annabella was like a sister and Charlie a brother. Her mind faltered on Joel. She had schooled herself not to think of him and had been successful for the most part. He had been away for so long and belonged to another part of her life. A life when she had been young and carefree...

She tossed her head, dismissing the urge to reminisce, and wishing Nathan had not mentioned the

Bradburys at all today. Their unusual relationship was the result of Eden's great-grandfather Morley being the head gamekeeper of the estate, a position he passed onto his son. All of Eden's family had worked for the estate since her great-grandfather was a lad. Eden's own mother had been lady's maid to Annabelle's grandmother and mother, and her father had been their coachman. She had grown up playing in the estate grounds, and being an only child, she had enjoyed her special friendship with the children of the Hall. It seemed natural to follow her mother into the role of lady's maid and companion to the female Bradbury.

On her great-grandfather's retirement he gained, as recognition to his family's devoted service, a pension, cottage and three acres on free hold land at the edge of the estate in what was known as Bottom Wood. They, as small landholders, had a respectable position in the small local village.

She looked up as the girls ran to her with Nathan walking behind, his expression one of apology.

Lillie gave her a small posy of wildflowers and Eden kissed the top of her fair head. 'Thank you dearest. Come now, it's time to go home. You need to change your damp clothes and there are chores to be done.'

'Can we not do them today, Mam?' Josephine pouted, dragging her feet as they collected the basket and blanket. Her dark hair hung in untidy strands down her back.

'I've explained this before. The animals need to be fed. Would you like to go without your supper?' Eden frowned at her eldest daughter, the one inclined to argue. 'Compared to most children you do very little. Be grateful.'

'Don't be harsh with her, Eden,' Nathan murmured, taking the basket from her. 'I'm sorry I spoilt your day.'

'You didn't, not really.' She sighed and forced a smile, trying to recapture the happiness she felt only an hour before. She knew the ghosts of her past walked in the shadows. They had tried very hard for nearly seven years to ignore them, but her leaving the Hall last week had stirred up memories and emotions long thought dead.

They strolled away from the gurgling river and into the shade of the beech and sessile oak trees, following a well-worn path back to the cottage. Bottom Wood was a mixture of plantation and ancient woodland spread over many acres. Its cool interior was today lightened by the sunny weather, but Eden loved the forest in all seasons. Having been born in the cottage she had grown up playing in the wood, it was her home.

Nathan slid his hand into hers. 'Now you're a lady of leisure, what do you plan to do with your days?'

'Huh!' She nudged him with her elbow. 'I'm sure I'll have enough to keep me occupied. For a start the cottage will get a good cleaning and a clear out, then I can plan to make more vegetable gardens. Grandfather needs a rest from taking care of everything. Some days he can barely stand for more than a few minutes and I know he worries that things have been allowed to slide into disarray.'

He nodded. 'I think he'll be very happy to have you home with him now.'

'Yes. I can keep an eye on him, and make sure he's not doing too much.'

She stared up into the leafy canopies above. As much as she adored being with Annabella, the

10

thought of staying home all the time lightened her heart. She could take care of her ailing grandfather, spend more time with the girls and work about the cottage, which in turn would ease Nathan's responsibilities. He worked hard enough at the Bradbury's cotton mill, where he was a manager, without having to work in the cottage as well because she was always at the Hall.

They rounded a bend and the wooden cottage, dull with age, came into view, nestled amongst overgrown gardens, an orchard and the backdrop of tall dark trees. Sitting out front on a wicker chair and smoking a clay pipe was her grandfather and opposite him was old Barney, a groom from the Hall. Both held pots of home brewed ale. They were deep in conversation and wore worried expressions until the girls skipped towards them and then they sat back and turned with a smile. The girls chatted a moment before running inside to change.

Still holding hands, Eden and Nathan stopped and greeted the visitor. 'How is everything with you, Barney?' Eden asked him.

'Well, lass, thank yer.' Barney glanced at her grandfather, who slightly shook his head.

Eden stiffened. 'Is something the matter?'

Barney blinked rapidly. 'Nay-'

'Has something happened at the Hall?'

'Well, Mister Charlie is bad again with his chest. Yer know how he gets.'

Eden's heart beat a little faster. Charlie had always been sickly ever since they were children and last year was diagnosed with the dreaded consumption. She and Annabella spent most of their time with him, especially in the winter when cold weather kept him housebound.

'Poor man,' Nathan said. 'I only saw him in the village a few days ago and he looked extremely well.'

'Aye,' Barney nodded, 'well he an' the Master got caught in the rain that evening an'…an' they've both been in bed ever since.'

'Both?' Eden blinked in surprise. 'Are they very bad?'

'The doctor's been each day. I've never known the Master to be poorly in the entire time I've been at the estate, which is near on thirty years.'

'Why didn't someone come and tell me?' She fumed.

'All them inside have been kept busy with two of them to care for.'

'So how ill are they?'

'Right bad from what I hear. The Master must be, to stay abed for days. Yer know him as well as me and he's not one for staying indoors.'

'Why wasn't I called? They know I sit with Charlie when he's unwell. I could have helped care for both of them. Has Mrs Fleming engaged nurses?'

Barney's eyes widened at her onslaught. 'Eh, I don't know what happens in the house, lass.'

'I must visit them.' Eden ignored Nathan's hand squeeze. Did he expect her to forget the family now Annabella had married and moved away? She let go of his hand and went to stand by the open doorway. The girls' chattering drifted down from the attic room above.

'That's kind of yer, lass.' Barney stood, placing his ale by his feet. 'I'd best be getting back, not that I'm eager to.'

Eden, about to call the girls to do their chores, paused and looked suspiciously back at Barney. 'Why's that then?'

Grandfather straightened in his chair and removed the pipe from his mouth. 'Take care then, Barney. Call again next week if you've a mind to.'

Her grandfather's diversion was wasted as Eden took a step forward. 'What else is happening up at the Hall, Barney?'

'Nowt lass.' The groom's weather-beaten face paled and he tugged his flat cap down over his brow as he patted her grandfather's shoulder. 'I'll be off now, Horatio. Good afternoon to yer all.'

Eden's hand shot out and stopped him from walking away. She knew he was hiding something. 'Barney?'

'Eden!' Grandfather and Nathan barked at the same time.

Her gaze didn't waver from Barney's. 'What is it?'

He sighed heavily and looked down at his boots. '*He*'s arriving this evening.'

'Who?' She whispered, but she knew already the man he referred to. There was only one man that the whole estate hated.

'Mr Clifton.'

She heard Nathan's grunt of anger and wearily closed her eyes. *He* was back.

Roland Clifton, the Bradbury's cousin. The man she hated with every ounce of her being. The man who had turned her world upside down, who haunted her dreams and rode the shadows at her back.

'Eden.' Nathan stood close, his hand on her waist.

'I'm fine, dearest.' She looked into his steady eyes and drew strength from him. 'He-he's been before and our paths haven't crossed. I'm sure it'll be the same this time.'

13

Grandfather coughed and she turned to him, but Barney's wan face made her stop. 'He-he *is* only staying a short time, isn't he?'

'I'm afraid not, lass. From what I heard he's staying until the Master is well again.'

'Colonel Bradbury is the healthiest man I've ever known, a trifling little cold will not keep him to his bed, nor would it be reason enough to call Clifton to his side.' Her eyes narrowed on Barney, who dithered from foot to foot, and then to her grandfather. 'What else aren't you telling me?'

Horatio slowly pushed himself to his feet, his bones creaking with the effort. 'The Colonel has had some kind of heart seizure, lass. He's not long for this world, apparently.'

Eden jerked, instantly wanting to cry out a denial and at the same time wanting to race to the Hall. 'Why didn't you tell me the minute you found out? Why did I have to drag it out of you?'

Grandfather seemed to age even more before her eyes. 'Because I didn't want to ruin your picnic and because Clifton is set to stay at the Hall and manage the estate until Mister Joel returns home from the war in Africa. You knowing now or later wouldn't have altered the fact.'

She marched into the cottage and threw the blanket over the back of a chair. Her mind whirled with the sudden news. Clifton staying at the Hall, Joel coming home soon, the Colonel desperately ill and Charlie sick again too. For a moment she seemed unable to move as she thought of the things she must do. She had to wash and change before she went to the Hall, get supper ready...

'You're not going.' Nathan followed her inside, anger radiating from him.

14

With barely a look in his direction, she stoked up the fire to heat water. 'I'll do as I please, Nathan, and you'll have no say in it.'

He kicked the cottage door shut and strode to her, swivelling her around to face him. 'I'll not have it, you hear? If I say you're not going, then you're not!'

She stared at him as though he'd gone mad. Only once in all the years of her knowing him had she seen him so furious. Still, she wouldn't have him laying the law down, not after all this time. 'You may be my husband but those over at the Hall are a part of my family too.'

'It's all done with now. Annabella has gone!'

'I owe them my loyalty and they have it! That will never change.'

'You owe them nothing!' His face, that only hours ago was soft with contentment, now hardened, his lips thinned, his eyes narrowed. 'I'll not stand for you putting them first anymore. We're fed up with it.'

'Really?' She reared back, ripping her elbow out of his hold.

'Me, the girls and your grandfather have always been at the end of your affections and your time in regards to them lot.'

'That's not true!'

'Yes, it is and I'm sick and tired of it, Eden. We are your family not them. So, it will stop now. Today.'

She raised her chin. 'What do you plan to do then? Tie me up?'

'Don't tempt me.'

The girls crept down the attic ladder and edged around the room to the door. After one terrified look at their parents, they raced outside to start their chores.

Nathan turned back to her. 'See? Your obsession with the Bradburys make us row and it frightens the girls.'

'We don't have to row about them.'

'No, not as long as I give you the freedom to do as you please,' he scoffed.

'Nathan-'

'I don't understand you. I never have.' He sighed, sounding sad and lonely.

She took a step towards him, eager to comfort him, but he pinned her with a cold glare.

'I wouldn't have thought you so keen to be there at the Hall knowing that the bastard Clifton would be in attendance.'

Flinching, she looked away, back to the fire. 'I can visit the sick rooms without meeting him.'

'Do I have to beg?'

She swallowed, hearing the plea in his voice, hating him for making her feel so guilty and hating herself for making him that way. 'I can never give them up, Nathan. I'm sorry.'

He nodded. 'I've always known it. I guess I'm not man enough for you to want me more than them.'

The blood drained from her face and she felt cold all over. 'No!' She ran to him and threw her arms around him, holding him close. 'Never believe that. I love you. You mean so much to me. Where would I have been without you as my husband?'

Nathan gently disengaged himself from her embrace. 'Maybe you need to ask yourself that question more often.' He walked out of the cottage, not bothering to close the door.

She let out a deep breath. The day had started so beautifully and ended in a mess. Her head throbbed from the argument with Nathan and she wished to put

16

things right between them but all she could think of was Charlie and the Colonel being ill. The low rumble of her grandfather's voice drifted through the open door as he talked to the girls. Eden toyed with the idea of staying at home but, as ever, the pull of the Hall was too strong.

Chapter 2

Dusk was sketching fine lines on the countryside as Eden opened the gate leading from the deer park into Bradbury Hall's elaborate gardens. Securing the latch, she turned and paused. The beauty of the Hall never failed to move her. Its mullioned windows, the pillared porch entry, the pale limestone blocks, slate grey roof, all fitted so well together, giving the house an elegant dignity suitable to such a great family of the area.

Slipping through the gardens, Eden headed for one of the side entries situated near the rear servants' staircase. With luck, she would make it upstairs to Charlie's room without detection. No doors in the house squeaked, for the housekeeper, Mrs Fleming, swooped down on anything or anyone who didn't meet her exacting standards, and so, Eden was able to let herself into the house and ascend the dim narrow stairs up to the first floor unnoticed. Stopping before Charlie's bedroom door, she glanced around the empty, silent corridor. It wasn't as though she felt unwelcome, she knew she'd always be received by the Bradburys despite Annabella's leaving, no, it was more a sense of sadness of the times gone by. Why she was feeling so melancholy she didn't know, yet it lingered over her like a winter cloud.

The soft click of the handle turning was the only sound as Eden opened the door wider and stepped into the darkened room. Inwardly she tutted at this, knowing Charlie would hate such gloominess. She smiled instantly on seeing him in bed, propped up on pillows, reading by lamplight. At that moment, he glanced up, his hazel eyes she knew so well glazed over with indifference, obviously expecting a servant. They soon widened and lit up with delight as he recognised her.

'Eden!'

'Now then, my dearest, what's this I hear of you being ill and lingering in bed?' She grinned and hurried to him, eager to press her cheek to his in greeting, although, as always, he turned his mouth away from her. He'd told her before not to come close to him so as not to contract the disease wasting him away, but she refused. The very thought of him living the rest of his lift without an embrace was hideous.

'I'm so glad you have come.' Charlie's face, although pale and a little blue around the lips, looked as handsome as ever and his smile was just as cheeky as it'd always been. 'I've missed you.'

'And I, you.' Sitting on the edge of the bed, she held his right hand in both of hers and squeezed it gently. 'I'm sorry I didn't come sooner. I only just found out. No one sent me word.'

'I thought you'd wiped your hands of us.' He pouted like a small boy and then winked which spoilt the effect.

'As if I would!' Eden shook her head. 'Though I'll be giving Mrs Fleming a piece of my mind when I see her next. How dare she keep this from me.'

Charlie nodded and a lock of his thick chestnut brown hair flopped over his eyes. 'I thought as much.

I did tell her to send for you. Even Father asked for you. I fear Mrs Fleming is enjoying her sole rule of the house while Father is ill and Annabella gone.' He pushed the hair away, the glow leaving his eyes. 'Father is very sick. You must see him, you might help him regain his fight. He has never been one to give up.'

'I will, don't worry and Mrs Fleming best not get in my way.'

'I knew you would sort it all out. Your presence is needed here, always needed.' He paused. 'I shouldn't say such things. You have a family of your own.'

'Yes, I have, but then, I consider myself having two families.'

'We cannot ask Nathan to part with you anymore. We are selfish, all of us. We always have been.'

'Stop such nonsense talk. I'm fortunate to have so many people need me.'

Sighing, Charlie leant back against the pillows. 'I've never seen Father so ill. I knew it was bad when I heard that he'd sent for Joel and Annabella.'

Eden jerked straighter. 'Them both? But Annabella is sailing to the Mediterranean, she'll only fret when she hears the news, knowing she can't reach him for weeks.'

'I know, but Father was, and still is, distraught. God only knows when either of them can return. Joel is fighting in the middle of Africa somewhere. Of course, he'll want to return immediately, but will the army let him? They've got a job to do and won't allow their officers to leave them at random surely.'

She rubbed the back of his hand. 'Don't upset yourself, it'll do no good.'

They both looked to the door as it opened again and Mellor, Colonel Bradbury's batman entered. He checked his step on seeing Eden, but relief flashed in his eyes for a moment before his iron control reasserted itself. 'Mrs Harris. It is good to see you again.'

'And you, Mellor.'

'How do you fare in there?' Charlie asked. 'Is my father better?'

Mellor closed the door and came closer to the bed, his back as straight as though he was still on the military parade ground. 'I'm afraid not, Mister Charlie. A rum do it is and no mistake.' The catch in his voice was a sign that this hard, upright man wasn't handling the present situation at all well.

Charlie cleared his throat. 'Mrs Harris wishes to see the Colonel, is it possible or should she wait another day?'

'Tomorrow might be best, I think.' He turned an apologetic expression to Eden before addressing Charlie again. 'The doctor is with him at the moment, and the new nurse, which is why I had a moment to pop in and see you.' Mellor straightened even further. 'I told Mrs Fleming that hiring the nurse wasn't necessary, but she took no notice.' His nose twitched and two spots of colour reddened his cheeks. 'No nurse can care for the Colonel better than me, haven't I been doing the job for the last fifteen years or more?'

Charlie's lips quirked into a smile. 'You're right, of course, but perhaps the doctor believes a nurse will give you a rest now and then, for if you were to get sick too, who would look after the Colonel?'

Mellor raised his chin at the question. 'Why, I've not been unwell in ten years and the day I can't do my duty to the Colonel is the day they bury me six feet under. Now if you don't need me, Mister Charlie, I'll return to your father.'

Charlie nodded and once the door had closed behind the batman, he turned to grin at Eden. 'Poor old fellow.'

Eden frowned at the wooden door, again the sense of change haunting her. 'Such devotion is not good, Charlie. When your father does eventually die, Mellor won't know what to do with himself.'

Sighing, Charlie placed his book on the small mahogany table beside the bed. 'I fear many changes are coming, Eden.' He glanced at her and squeezed her hand. 'You know he's here, don't you? He arrived full of pomp and ceremony as though he owned the estate already.'

She swallowed, wishing he hadn't mentioned the man. 'Clifton will have to wish for three deaths for that to happen.'

'The chances are good, very good.'

Eden pulled away from him. 'Don't Charlie, don't say it.'

'Well unless Annabella has a child, Clifton gets it all. He knows Father and I aren't long for this world, one way or another, and he has a fine possibility that Joel will die on the battlefield. So, it only leaves him and Annabella's children. If she doesn't have any, well...'

Tutting in irritation, she stood and fiddled with the blankets. 'Of course, Annabella will have children. She is young and strong and look at Mr Carleton, he is healthy. He has four sisters and-'

'Enough.' Charlie took her hand again and kissed it. 'I shouldn't have said anything about it.' He smiled. 'I've missed your temper, your bickering, and your presence.'

She gave him a disparaging look. 'My temper is-'

'Delightful.' Suddenly, he appeared tired, drained.

'Go to sleep,' Eden whispered. 'I'll call again tomorrow.'

'You won't sleep here tonight?'

'No. I'll head off for home.'

'Is it wise? It's dark outside. Will Nathan be waiting for you at the gate? I don't want you taking any risks.'

'I'll be perfectly safe.' She kissed his cheek in farewell. 'Rest, eat Cook's good food and sleep.'

He caught her skirts as she made to leave. 'Will Nathan be waiting? The truth now.'

'I'm not certain. The girls-'

'He was angry you came here, wasn't he?'

Resisting the urge to slump onto the bed and pour her heart out, Eden tugged loose her skirts, pushed her shoulders back and walked towards the door. 'Nathan was – is fine about it, naturally. Now, go to sleep.' Before he had chance to utter another word, she slipped from the room and quietly closed the door.

'Mrs Harris!'

Eden jumped at the loud bark and twisted to stare at Mrs Fleming, who stood hands on hips at the end of the hallway. 'Good evening, Mrs Fleming.'

'This is not a good evening!' The older woman marched up and stood a few feet away, her plump face red and her beady eyes alight with burning anger. 'Why are you in this house?'

'I would think that obvious.'

'Mister Charlie has no need of you, thank you very much.' The housekeeper wagged a stubby fat finger in Eden's face. 'Your time here finished the moment Miss Annabella became Mrs Carleton.'

'I am still-'

'You are nothing, madam!' Mrs Fleming's hands curled into fists at her side.

'I see your true feelings have finally appeared.' Eden gave a wry smile. 'I gather they are long overdue. You've hidden your dislike for many years.'

'Yes, it was the happiest day of my life the day Miss Annabella married and you left this house.'

'Then your life must be so very empty if that was your happiest day.'

'I suffered enough of you lording over this house, being in Miss Annabella's confidences, thinking you were better than everyone else, but all the time you were a servant like the rest of us.'

Anger building, Eden leant closer to the fiery old hag. 'I care naught for your opinion or your jealousies, but you will respect the position I held in this house, which despite what you'd like to think, was far more than a servant. My time with Miss Annabella might be over, but there are other members of this family who do wish for my presence here and nothing you can say or do will alter the fact, and you well know it.'

'How dare you speak to me in that fashion.' Mrs Fleming gasped. 'I'll have you know-'

'I know more than enough about you, *Madam*!' Eden raised an eyebrow. 'I know all your little secrets. Shall I inform the Colonel of your sneaky habits? Of the housekeeping money you ferret from the accounts and slip into your own pocket? The sly bottles of wine or gin you have brought up from the cellar for your own table? The money you earn by selling wasted food to the beggars who come to the kitchen door? Shall I tell it all?'

Mrs Fleming's lips thinned into a tight blue line. 'You-You-'

24

'Good evening, Mrs Fleming.' With a sharp nod, Eden swished her skirts aside, swept around the older woman and marched downstairs.

Once outside, she sucked in a gulp of night air and wiped a shaky hand over her eyes. She hated confrontation, but the silly old mare had asked for it. For years, Eden had put up with the housekeeper's whispered unkind words behind her back and disapproving looks. However, Eden hadn't been aware of the depth of Fleming's dislike. Well, there's an end to it. She and Mrs Fleming would keep their distance even more now.

Walking across the grounds, she kept out of the shadows as much as possible, but the way to the gate led through a garden of clipped yew hedges and large conifers. Usually she wasn't frightened by night time noises or the dark, but tonight, after such a strange day and knowing Clifton was within the hall, she felt her skin tingle with every disturbance and sound.

She prayed that Nathan would be waiting for her at the gate like he normally did, but he wasn't there when she arrived. Shoulders slumping, she opened the gate and closed it again after herself. The large expanse of wood lay on the other side of an open field full of meadow flowers and long grasses. No figure walked across it in the moonlight.

Eden hesitated, both annoyed and upset that Nathan was being so childish by not meeting her. It wasn't his nature to be spiteful. Gathering her courage, and head held high and proud, she lifted her skirts and started across the field towards the dark woodland. On reaching the first trees, a figure stepped out beyond the shadows and she jumped in fright.

'You decided to come home then?' Nathan's face was unreadable in the muted light. 'Were you made welcome? Did they declare you were sorely missed?'

'Of course.' She walked, allowing her breath to slip out shakily. She'd never let him know how scared she was walking alone at night. But then, without speaking of it, he knew, that's why he always met her at the gate when she worked late.

'What if that had been someone else standing there and not me?' Nathan fell into step beside her. 'What would you have done?'

Tired and fed up with the events of the day, Eden stopped and turned to him. 'What would I have done?' she barked. 'I would have screamed my bloody head off, you silly man! And then cursed you for not meeting me.'

Nathan stood and as moonlight whispered through the trees and landed on his face, he smiled. 'Aye, you bloody would.'

She wanted to sink into his arms but remained still. 'Do you forgive me?'

He took a deep breath and let it our slowly. 'Aye. Only, I want limits set this time, Eden. You're not living over there half the time like before. I want you home.'

She tucked her hand into his arm. 'They are sick and need me.' When he baulked, she put her finger to his lips to silence any protests. 'Once they are well again, I will not go there as much, I promise.'

He nodded and they walked on a bit. 'Did you see *him*?'

Eden leant her head against his shoulder as they strolled. 'No, and I hope I never do. However, the time will come, and I must be prepared for it.'

Chapter 3

At the small sound coming from the bed, Eden lifted her head from reading the book on her lap and turned to peer at the Colonel's pallid face. An eyelid flickered then was still. Mellors paused in his task of polishing the Colonel's uniform brass at a small table in the corner of the room and watched the older man sleeping.

The nurse, Pettigrew, who had been dozing in her chair shifted, snorted and then sprang awake as though she'd been shaken. 'Nay.' She blinked, straightened her starched apron and leant over her patient with a scowl.

'He's fine,' Eden whispered, placing her book on the small bedside table.

Pettigrew's scowl deepened. 'His colour isn't so good.' She turned to Mellors. 'This room has grown cold.'

Mellors rose, his expression stiff. 'I told you we needed more wood, but you said we weren't to make the room too hot to give him a fever.'

'Aye, but I didn't say to keep it as cold as winter's night!' She swished her skirts out of the way and headed for the door. 'I'll go down and prepare a tray for the Colonel should he wake, I can't be trusting anyone else to do it, can I?'

Mellors headed for the door too. 'And I'll get some wood and keep the room as the Colonel likes it, for you can't be *trusted* to know his needs as well as me!'

Together they bustled out of the door leaving silence to settle like a cloak around the room. Eden checked that their whispered argument hadn't woken the man they fought over. In sleep the colonel looked younger, a lot more like Joel too. Joel. Eden sighed whenever she thought of her childhood sweetheart, the man who'd she lived for, the one who despite their social differences made her feel so special, so much his...

She turned away from the bed and walked to the large window overlooking the gardens. Below a gardener clipped a hedge. Eden watched him work, but her mind was recalling her childhood, the happy carefree days when they were all together. How she and Annabella roamed the woods, searching for the boys when they were desperate to leave the girls behind and do some serious fishing, or when they had all gone on picnics by the river and played hide and seek.

Hugging herself, she gazed out over the horizon towards where the small town of Gargrave lay in the north and then looked to the northwest to the wind swept moors. Heavy grey clouds hung low, as though ready to wipe from memory the beautiful weather of yesterday. It'd been a cold day like today when she last saw Joel.

How had the years flown by so quickly? Seven years. Seven years since she told him to take care as he headed off to the demands of the army. He had known she loved him, not as a brother, not like she loved Charlie, but as a woman loved a man. Yet, what could be done? With him suddenly becoming an officer, it was as though their social differences had jumped up and made itself plain for the first time in their lives. Joel was an officer, the heir to the estate and she…she his sister's companion, the daughter of servants. He couldn't marry her, he had to find some suitable daughter from a wealthy family of pedigree.

A noise came from the bed again, breaking through her memories. She turned and smiled at the Colonel who lay looking at her. 'How do you feel, sir?'

'Like…' he licked his dry lips, 'like death warmed up.'

She smiled and he gave her a slow wink. 'Well, gather your strength because the nurse and Mellors will be back any moment.' She added another pillow behind his head and then poured out a glass of water and helped him to sip it.

'I'm tired, Eden, so very tired.'

'I know.' She made him comfortable again by adjusting his pillows.

'I've never been tired before, not like this.'

'You'll get better soon.'

'I won't.' He sighed deeply and the age once more lined his face. 'I'm rather annoyed my body has done this to me. There's so much left undone…'

'Undone?' Eden grinned at him as she sat back on the chair. 'I would've thought, sir, that you've lived a very full life.'

He shook his head and lifted a hand for her to take. The large hand, which had once been so strong, now lay feeble in hers and it saddened her that such a man as he, someone who always seemed invincible, was now bedridden. His fighting, happy spirit had gone and replaced by the melancholy of the dying.

'I've never said sorry, Eden.'

She stared at him, puzzled. 'Sorry? Whatever for? You have no need to say sorry to me for anything.'

'You don't know that I know…' He glanced away towards the door.

The fine hairs on the back of her neck stood up and her heartbeat raced only to suddenly slow down again in dread. 'You know what?' she whispered.

'Your secret. The secret you share with your husband and, unbeknown, with me.' He paused, a spasm of pain crossed his face making him suck in a breath and close his eyes for a moment.

He knew. Eden fell back against the chair, the warmth leaving her face. 'How did you know?'

'I saw him coming out of the woods, adjusting his trousers, wiping the blood off his face from the scratch marks.' The Colonel shuddered. 'He didn't see me. I was out riding, but Jupiter had thrown a shoe and I'd dismounted to check his leg. After he had gone from sight, I hurried into the woods to search for whatever servant or maid he'd attacked. Then I saw you in the distance stumbling towards the cottage. Your hair hung down your back…your skirt dirty…'

Silence lengthened between them. Eden was too shocked to speak, to think clearly. The memory of that horrible day wanted to come back and relive itself. But, as always, she pushed it away, buried it deep, never wanting to acknowledge what had happened to her within her beautiful wood.

'I'm sorry. I should have done more… especially after all the comfort you've been to my Annabella.'

She jumped to her feet; her hands busy at the bed-covers. 'There's nothing for you to be sorry about. It wasn't your fault.'

'Clifton is my nephew. It would have killed my sister Ada to know of his true nature, of his evil acts. I couldn't denounce him without bringing shame to Ada, and she's never been strong. However, I have put off most of his visits best I can, leaving only the odd times when I could find no excuse. When-when he is here, I've always tried to keep him so busy that he could never find the time to-' His face contorted with pain and he wheezed for breath.

Eden stood over him, frustrated at not being able to do anything. 'Rest now, sir. Sleep. You mustn't tire yourself.'

His pale blue eyes searched her face. 'I want my boy back...'

Her hands stilled over the blankets. 'Joel will be home as soon as he can.'

'It's been too long...' He gasped, clutching at his chest.

'At least you saw him two years ago in South Africa.'

'My last trip away.'

'For the rest of us it's been much longer.'

The colonel closed his eyes. 'Do... you forgive me?'

Gripping the blankets in her fists, she swallowed, gathering her strength. 'Yes.'

She glanced up as the door opened and Mellors entered carrying a timber box full of short logs.

'He was awake?' Mellors placed the box by the hearth and gently stirred the low fire. 'I missed him being awake.'

'It was only for a minute,' she lied and went to stand beside him, holding her hands out to the new flames.

'I got held up by that fancy piece of uselessness!' Mellors fumed, stacking the logs.

Eden's stomach churned. 'Clifton.'

'Aye, *him*,' he whispered with a glance towards the bed. 'He's been out riding the Colonel's good hunter, it was lathered in sweat. Stupid man. Then he waited until I was loaded up before stopping me in the middle of the yard to ask about the Colonel's progress. He could see I had wood to take back. I bet he wanted the fire to go out and the cold to kill his uncle off. Why, if he ever gets his hands on this place, I'll be marching straight out the door.'

'You won't be alone in that.' Eden shivered. 'Did you see Master Charlie?'

'No, but they say in the kitchens he's much better today.' Mellors stood and wiped his hands clean on a piece of flannel he kept in his pocket. 'You popping in to see him?'

'No.' She went to the straight-backed chair she'd been sitting in, collected her shawl and wrapped it around her shoulders. 'It looks like rain and I don't want to be caught in it. Will you see Master Charlie later and let him know I'll spend tomorrow with him?'

'Aye lass, of course.'

'He was fast asleep when I poked my head around the door earlier, but I promised Nathan I wouldn't sleep here anymore so I can't stay.'

'You do right, lass. I'll take care of them both. You go on home, rest easy. I'll send word if there's any change.'

She patted his hand. 'Thank you.' With a last lingering look at the Colonel, she slipped out of the room.

She hurried down the dim corridor, her footsteps faltering by Charlie's door. She longed to go into him, but dared not. He would see her face and know there was something wrong.

Ahead a door opened on the right and Clifton stepped out. Eden froze, staring at him with revulsion and fear.

'Why, it's the lovely Eden, the temptress.' Clifton drawled in his London accent. Since she'd last seen him, he gained extra weight around his middle and his slick black hair had receded more from the forehead, giving his head a dome shape. Fleshy jowls elongated his face so that it seemed he had no neck, just a head on fat rounded shoulders. Once, when younger, he'd been a handsome man, but his hectic, hedonistic social life and vicious nature had stripped him bare of all gentility.

Determined not to let him see her emotions if she could help it, Eden tilted her chin higher, her stare icy. 'Mr Clifton.' She inclined her head and made to pass him, but his hand shot out and cruelly gripped her upper arm.

'We meet again, Mrs Harris.' His small eyes narrowed as an evil grin revealed yellowing teeth. 'It is always a pleasure.'

He was not much taller than she, but he was immensely strong, a strength she had experienced before. She glared into his face. 'You are hurting my arm.'

Instead of releasing her, he brought her closer to his body and her insides shrivelled. 'I'd never hurt you, my dear,' he murmured into her ear. 'You know I regard you most highly.' Yet his action belied those words when he threw her casually away from him and then wiped down his jacket as though she had dirtied his immaculate attire.

Eden picked up her skirts and fled past him only to stop as he called her name. Slowly she glanced back over her shoulder.

'Did you know I was here?' Clifton smiled.

Blinking, she hovered by the servant's staircase. 'What do you mean?'

'Are you stupid?' He tugged on his left earlobe, looking so at ease. 'I asked if you knew that I had arrived.'

'I was told yesterday.'

'And you still came?'

'The Colonel and Charlie need me.'

'That was the only reason?' He frowned. 'You didn't come wanting to see me?'

She swallowed. 'Why-why would I want to see you?'

'You do not think of me then?'

'No...'

'Pity. I think of you a great deal.'

Eden swayed and wondered if she'd faint at his feet.

Clifton straightened and shook his head a little. 'Right then. Well, it was good to see you again. I am pleased you are still about the house.' He spun on his heel and marched up the corridor to descend the main staircase.

Had she heard correctly? Was she dreaming? Was he mad? How had he changed from being evil to civil within the space of a heartbeat? Carefully, she stepped down the narrow steep servants' stairs and made her way out of the house, her mind whirling. The last time Clifton had been at the house she had not seen him except through a window. She made sure to keep well away from the areas he used in the house and gardens and done so successfully. They'd not met, and she'd been able to continue her life by putting him out of her mind.

Now it had changed. Instinct told her that he would figure in her life again. She shuddered and pressed her hand against her mouth to stifle a moan.

Picking up her skirts, she ran through the garden to the deer park and across the fields to the wood. Once inside the dim cool interior, she sucked in a breath and forced herself to calm down. Her gaze strayed to the left. A hundred yards or so up a slight incline the wood opened into a small clearing, that spot had been her favourite place to sit on a sunny day. It'd been seven years since she'd walked there. Eden took one step in that direction before fear stopped her. Not yet, she couldn't go there just yet.

'Mama!' Josephine and Lillie ran down the path from the cottage and flung themselves into her out-stretched arms.

'My petals.' She kissed the top of their heads. 'Did you enjoy school?'

'I got an apple from Mr Johnson for reading beautifully.' Josephine took Eden's hand. 'You're home early. I'm glad.'

Eden squeezed her fingers before taking Lillie's hand too. 'Yes, I am and we've got the whole afternoon and night together. What shall we do?'

'Make gingerbread!' Lillie squealed; her grey eyes alight. 'Or currant bread.'

'No.' Her sister scowled. 'Let Mama read to us by the fire.'

The first drop of rain fell through the canopy of branches overhead and landed on Eden's cheek. 'We should hurry, or we'll be spending the night sneezing and coughing from colds.'

Josephine glanced over her shoulder. 'Mama, someone comes.'

Eden stopped and turned around. Silhouetted in the wood opening by the light of the fields beyond was a running figure. A woman waved to them, but Eden couldn't make out who it was in the dwindling light.

'Eden! Wait up.'

'It's Jane from the Hall, Mama,' Josephine said.

They walked down the path to meet the lumbering young woman, who still wore her kitchen apron and maid's cap. Jane, on reaching them, bent over to catch her breath.

'Whatever is the matter, Jane?' Eden watched the plump maid straighten and fill her lungs with air.

Jane looked at the girls and tried to compose herself but failed miserably. Her face crumbled and she twisted the apron in her hands. 'You've got to come back.'

Dread clamped Eden's heart. 'What's happened?'

'The Colonel…he's dead.'

Chapter 4

Huddled in her black cloak, Eden gazed at the mourners standing around the open grave, they resembled a flock of crows. Gentle rain fell from steel grey clouds, as it had done on and off for four days. In front of her was the black wrought iron fence, which divided the deceased Bradburys from the rest of the estate's dead. Only immediate family, which wasn't many, stood inside the small fenced off area, the rest of the mourners respectfully stayed on the outer, careful not to tread on recently dug graves for the ill weather had made the ground thick with mud.

Beside her, Nathan shifted his weight from foot to foot. Lifting his head, he smiled at her in a measure of sympathy and she linked her hand through his arm for comfort. The vicar continued to address his audience, God and the lowering sky alternatively, sinfully keeping them out in the cold longer than necessary. Eden wanted him done for back at the Hall, Charlie sat alone mourning his father.

Clumps of wet earth clattered down onto the coffin and the noise was so final Eden had to turn her head away. Her gaze sought the angel sculpture sitting on top of Amelia Bradbury's high tombstone. The Colonel was joining his wife. Her heart ached. Never would they hear the Colonel's strident laughter echoing the hallways, see him canter off at the head of a hunt meet or watch his eyes brighten when Annabella embraced him.

Her gaze roamed over the heads of the gathered to linger on the small timbered church, built by the Colonel's father for the family and estate's personal use, to save them all trudging the miles to Gargrave every Sunday.

A collective sigh alerted her back to the situation in hand and she also sighed in relief as the vicar, having finished his duties, was now shaking hands and murmured platitudes to Clifton, his widowed mother, one or two great aunts and some very distant cousins. The main members of the family, the Colonel's children, were keenly missed by their absence.

'I'll be getting back to the mill, Eden.' Nathan kissed her cheek and cautiously glanced towards Clifton. 'You'll be all right?'

She smiled and nodded. 'Yes, of course. Mellors said I can share the gig with him. I don't know how he managed to get it, but at least it saves me walking or riding in the cart with the staff.'

At that moment, Mellors came to stand at her side and shook hands with Nathan. 'How's it at the mill then, Nathan?'

'So far nowt has changed, but I bet it doesn't stay that way for long if *he's* around.' Nathan jerked his head in the direction of Clifton. 'Bradbury Mill is no place for the likes of him. We'll strike if he starts messing about. He was throwing his weight around the other morning, giving orders not needed and carrying on as though we don't know our jobs.'

'Master Charlie will come good again, and send that one packing.' Mellors murmured, his eyes full of hostility.

38

'I hope so for all our sakes. Right then, I'll be off.' Nathan took a step, but Eden halted him.

'I don't know what time I'll be home. Charlie...'

Nathan nodded, his expression solemn. 'Aye...'

She watched him walked away, his shoulders hunched against the misty rain that was rolling in as though it was mid-winter and not the end of summer. A sense of foreboding came over her.

They returned to the sombreness of the Hall, the servants quickly changing out of their Sunday best and into uniforms while the family and acquaintances sipped sherry by the fire in the drawing room.

Eden escaped upstairs and after a slight knock entered Charlie's room. He sat in a leather winged-back chair by a roaring fire with a tartan blanket over his knees.

He held out his hand to her. 'How was it?'

'As expected.' She placed his hand against her cold cheek.

'You're frozen. Come closer to the fire.' He grabbed the iron poker and thrust at the logs, which erupted them into a fierce blaze while she took off her gloves, hat and cloak. Her black skirts weren't too damp.

She sat in the chair opposite him and watched the flames flicker up the chimney.

Charlie replaced the poker and sat back. 'You look pensive.'

'Funerals do that to you don't they.'

'I believe so. Such dreary occasions. I suppose downstairs is a mass of circling vultures, betting on the next Bradbury death.'

'Well, to me they look like a lot of old crows more than vultures, but hopefully their conversation is of a lighter subject.'

39

'Not with Clifton acting the host.' He shifted in his chair, his fist scrunching up the edge of the blanket. 'I'm afraid I will have to disappoint him and not die as he wishes.'

'Good. Then he can leave and hopefully never return.'

'Poor Roland, he never did get on your good side.'

Eden shivered. How many times had she come close to telling Charlie everything? Yet why give him the burden of knowing. He had more than enough to contend with. 'Or yours either.'

'No. The poor fellow was often left behind, wasn't he?' Charlie wrinkled his nose. 'I believe he hated coming here for the holidays as a child. We called him Rolly-Polly. Children are dreadfully mean.'

'Clifton was mean in return.'

'He was useless at everything, was he? Couldn't shoot well, swim across the river, climb trees or put a horse to the jump. Remember? Joel couldn't be bothered with him. Never had any time back then for fools, did our Joel, and I doubt that has changed. Clifton certainly hasn't.'

'Clifton might be a fool but he's a clever fool in some ways.'

Charlie nodded, his fingers picking at the blanket's thread. 'Yes, a little cruel at times. I'll never forget that day he whipped the sheep dog from Home Farm. If Joel hadn't knocked Clifton down, I would have.' Charlie gave her a wry smile. 'It would've been my first fight, but Joel, as always, wouldn't allow anyone to do a job he could do himself and so saved me the effort of blooding my hand or nose.'

Eden watched the flames. Joel had always been there for them, their knight, their hero and protector. Then he had gone, leaving a big hole in everyone's lives and casting his little band of followers adrift. 'You have to show a presence downstairs soon, Charlie. Clifton has to leave. He will feel less confident of his place here if he knows you are up and about.'

'Is he so very bad? We know he is unpleasant company, but he's come here to help us, to take care of the estate.'

'There was no need for him to come. Your father trusted his steward and you trust him too, don't you? Has Parkinson ever made you doubt his service?'

'No, of course not. Parkinson has run the estate many times while the family has been away.'

'Exactly, so why is Clifton needed?'

'Eden-'

'Open your eyes, Charlie.' Unable to contain her agitation, she rose and walked to the window. The rainy scene outside was as bleak as she felt.

'What is it? Why this sudden aversion to Clifton's presence?'

She didn't turn around. 'I've always had it, you know that. Even as children I didn't like him.'

'I have very little of my family left at the moment, Eden. Clifton, for all his faults, is my cousin.'

'Must that blind you to his sins?' she whispered.

'Do you know of something that I don't?'

Eden held her breath. Could she tell him? Should she? Slowly she turned and faced him. He stared at the flames and in profile his gauntness seemed intensified, the cheekbones prominent. In that moment she saw him as an old man, his flesh wasted by disease, the young handsome man of their youth gone. He didn't deserve to be yoked to her troubles, her secrets. In a rush of affection, she hurried to him and hugged him. 'I'm sorry.'

He patted her hand, kissed her cheek. 'I love you like my own sister. Your opinions are always valued by me.'

'I know.'

'However, you are right. Until Joel returns, I am in charge, not Clifton.' He stood up and threw the blanket off. 'I'll go down now. Will you help me?'

She stared up at him. 'Now? Today? I didn't mean at this minute, I meant soon.'

'Why put it off. It's my father's wake, I should go down. No more can I hide in my room with my books and let everyone else take responsibility.' He went into the small dressing room and changed his jacket. When he came back out, he carried polished black shoes and sat on the bed. 'Will you help me put these on?'

'You don't have to do this.' She went to help him take off his slippers and put on his shoes. 'I should learn to be silent.'

'Silent? You? I've never heard of anything so absurd.' He grinned.

'Do you feel well enough? I won't have you tiring yourself.'

'I'll only stay down there for a few minutes, just to show my face. Dispel some rumours of my imminent demise.'

She stood and straightened her skirts out. They looked at each other. This was the first step in a new life for them all. Charlie had to assert his authority now his father was gone.

Charlie rose and although pale, his eyes seemed brighter than before. 'You will stay with me.'

'Always.' Linking arms, they left the room and went downstairs.

The drawing room chatter reached them in the hall, and Charlie paused to take a deep breath and head high, he escorted her into the throng. Acquaintances, shocked at his sudden appearance, quickly closed their gaping mouths and hurriedly spoke of their pleasure at seeing him.

With Charlie at her side, Eden took courage and looked for Clifton. It was a long-held habit of hers to try and find out his whereabouts when in close proximity to him. Too many times in the past had he delighted in springing out from nowhere and frightening her. He stood beside the blazing fireplace, cradling a small glass of whiskey. Beside him on the lounge were his mother, Ada and his elderly aunts. Over their heads, Clifton stared at Eden. Laughter now masked his origin shock at seeing them walked into the room. He inclined his head to her in salute. He knew of her scheme.

Mixing with old friends and talking about his father gave Charlie a new lease of life. His few minutes of showing his face turned into an hour. Eden stayed beside him, plying him with tea and cake and watching for signs of tiredness. The whole time she was aware of Clifton prowling the room, chatting, drinking and eyeing her at every available moment.

When there was a lull of conversation, Eden bent to whisper in Charlie's ear. 'Perhaps you should return upstairs for a rest.'

He nodded and smiled. 'Don't want to overdo it, do I?'

'No, dearest.' She helped him up from the wide cream and gold striped sofa and waited as he said his goodbyes.

'Escaping I see?' Clifton had come from behind without her knowing.

She turned to give him a cool look. 'Charlie is tired.'

A footman strolled by with a tray of drinks and Clifton casually selected one. 'Do you care for his every need, I wonder?'

'Only a slug like you would think such a thing.'

Clifton sipped his drink then grinned. 'You know, I heard a most interesting piece of news this morning.'

'I'm delighted for you. Excuse me.' She gathered her skirts, eager to be beside Charlie again, who was now kissing the hands of his aunt Ada and great aunts.

'My mother will be so pleased.'

Confused, Eden paused and frowned. 'Pardon?'

A wicked glint fired his pale eyes. 'My mother has always wanted to be a grandmother.'

'I don't follow you.'

'I hear you have a child, a daughter who is of the correct age…to be mine.'

Something infinite died inside Eden. 'W-What a fantasy you weave, Clifton.'

He pushed his shoulders back, delight flushing his features, and for a terrifying moment, she thought he was going to announce it to the room. 'I see by your face that I am right in my thinking, so it's not such a fantasy after all, hey?'

'You-you are deluded. She…my daughter isn't yours. The thought is ridiculous!'

'I am not so fooled, precious Eden.' Clifton leaned closer, washing her with his whiskey breath. 'Your eldest daughter is mine and you cannot prove otherwise. I'm annoyed with myself for not thinking of this earlier. Six years of fathering I've missed out on.' He sounded as if he cared, but she saw the cruel glint in his eyes. He had missed out on years of hurting her in some way.

She took a step back, fear clutching at her insides. 'My husband is my daughter's father. *You* cannot prove otherwise.'

'I was also told your daughter arrived only seven months after your marriage to Harris. Interesting. I wonder how the court will see it?' His mocking expression made her legs weaken.

'You wouldn't...'

He flashed yellow teeth. 'Ahh, now my dear, some things are meant to be. I actually think I would make an excellent father, don't you agree?'

'You come anywhere near us and I'll—'

'You'll what my dear?' His gaze roamed over her body. 'I can't believe...' his voice dropped to a whisper. 'I can't believe I have left it so long since I sampled your body again. Most remiss of me.'

'Eden?' Charlie was beside her and grasped her elbow. 'What is it, you look ill.'

'Needs some air I think, cousin,' Clifton murmured. 'Funerals are so taxing.'

Groping her way out of the room, Eden was aware of the stares directed at her and tried to pull herself together.

'Eden, perhaps you should lie down?' Full of concern, Charlie helped her up the staircase.

Halfway up, she hesitated. Josephine. God, Clifton wanted her daughter, *knew* about her beautiful daughter! She had to go home, check to see if Josephine was all right, to touch her and affirm she was safe.

'What happened?' Charlie demanded. 'What did Clifton say to you?'

She gazed at him, her dearest Charlie, and for once wished that his brother was here instead. Joel would sort this out, he'd throw Clifton out on his head, but Charlie, sick Charlie, could never do such a thing.

'I have to go home, I must. Now.' She turned to go down, but Charlie's grip held her.

'Talk to me, Eden. Please.' His eyes implored her.

'I will, but not now.' She pulled free and, after sending him an apologetic look, she tore down the stairs and out through the front doors. Rain pelted her bare head and carriage drivers stared at her as she raced around the side of the house and into the gardens.

Lifting her skirts high, she ran all the way home. A stitch pained her side and her hair had come loose. The tall trees of the wood dripped a tattoo of their own as rain seeped through the canopy above. The path made from fallen vegetation trodden in over the years was spongy under her feet. She uttered a sob of relief when the cottage loomed before her through the murky grey of the rain. Home. Safety.

Eden burst into the cottage, startling her grandfather so much he dropped his pipe out of his mouth.

'Eden!'

Wildly she searched the room for her girls, for Josephine. 'Where is she?' She nearly screamed at her grandfather.

'Who, for heaven's sake. What the 'ell is wrong?' He stared at her as though she'd lost her mind, while bending down to collect his pipe from the floor.

'Josephine!' Eden rushed to the bottom of the attic ladder. 'Josephine!'

'She's at school, you silly 'apporth.' Grandfather pushed himself up from his chair. 'What's happened?'

Eden ran back to the door intent on running all the way to Gargrave and the little village school.

'Stop,' Grandfather shouted, halting her with her hand on the latch. 'Sit!'

'I can't, I have to get to Josephine.'

'Is she ill, in danger?' He hobbled closer, his eyes, as blue as a summer sky pinned her to the spot. 'Tell me.'

'Clifton knows.' Just saying the words, knocked the wind out of her and she slumped against the door, shaking.

'Bastard.' Grandfather gathered her into his arms and then led her to the sofa by the fire. 'You need a brandy.'

'I-'

'You'll have a brandy and speak of what's occurred.' He shuffled over to the range against the far wall and from a cupboard built to the side of the small window, he brought out a half-full bottle.

Eden twisted her hands together, torn between staying and dashing for the door. The heat from the fire caused her skirts to steam.

'Drink this.' Grandfather pressed the little glass into her hands and watched her drink.

The brandy blazed a trailed down her throat. She hated the taste of it, but soon the warmth hit her stomach and spread.

'So, he knows then.'

'Yes.' She nodded, suddenly wanting to curl up into a ball and hide. 'I told him it was untrue, but he doesn't believe me.'

'A man like him will only believe what he wants anyway.' Grandfather sagged back down on his chair. 'What else did he say?'

'He indicated that he wants Josephine…' For a moment Eden thought she would be sick. 'He said the courts…the courts would believe him…'

Grandfather swore violently and grabbing the poker, jabbed aggressively at the coals in the fire. 'He's the type who would do such a thing. Tear a family apart.'

'I can't let him take her.'

'He needs to prove it first and that won't be easy. You married Nathan soon after Clifton...'

'It'll be my word against his.' Eden stared down at the glass in her hands. 'He has position and money on his side. They will believe him.' A black mist seemed to penetrate her mind, numbing her from thinking and feeling, sheltering her from the hideous thoughts of Clifton taking her daughter.

'It won't come to that. We'll talk it over with Nathan tonight, work out a plan.'

'Nathan. Oh Grandfather, Nathan will be devastated.' Tears ran down her cheeks. 'He loves her like his own. Adores her. The gossip will kill him, you know how private he is and the girls-'

'Nay, my lass, don't take on.' He reached over an arthritic hand and patted her knee. 'We'll get it sorted. I promise.'

She nodded, finding strength from him. 'Likely Clifton just wanted to scare me.'

'Aye, that might be all it is.' Grandfather took the glass from her. 'Go get changed and then walk to meet the girls coming home. It'll be a nice surprise for them.'

'Yes.' Eden stood and stepped towards the ladder.

'You should stay away from the Hall for a while. I know Master Charlie will want you with him now the Colonel has gone, but Josephine is more important.'

'Of course.' The thought of going near the hall while Clifton was there made her skin crawl.

As Eden placed her foot on the first rung, a loud pounding sounded on the door. She looked at her grandfather. 'Are you expecting someone?'

'Nay, who'd come out in this foul weather?' He grabbed his walking stick from near his chair and hobbled over to open the door. A blast of cold wind blew in, which made smoke billow back down the chimney and for a moment Eden couldn't see who was on the doorstep.

'You!' Grandfather's bark filled the cottage.

Eden's eyes widen as Clifton, wearing a long, dark brown coat and a hat pulled down low, stepped past the old man and into the cottage. His eyes surveyed the room before resting on Eden. 'So, where is she? Where is my daughter!'

Chapter 5

Major Joel Bradbury raised his field binoculars and scanned the African plain before him, shimmering in a heat haze. The dry brown grasses rippled as though swept by a giant hand. Beneath him, his horse Fidget stepped sideways for no particular reason, hence his name, and Joel clamped his knees in tighter to steady him. Fidget had been looked over by most officers who couldn't abide a horse that wouldn't stand still, but Joel had felt something stir within him when he gazed into the gelding's large liquid brown eyes. What the other officers had not realised was that despite his restlessness, Fidget, once urged to, could out gallop any other horse in the regiment. This speed had saved Joel's life on more than one occasion.

A spot on the crest of the valley caught Joel's attention. He studied it as it moved and then soon became clear as a horse and rider. His man? Tensing, Joel squinted through the binoculars, ignoring the heat burning through his uniform. The rider thundered down the slope and cantered towards where Joel and his scouting party waited.

Bertram. Good. Releasing a breath of relief, Joel swept the binoculars past his scout and up the valley, checking for Boers. 'Tell the men to mount up, Haversham.'

'Sir.' The young First Lieutenant, standing at Fidget's right flank, saluted and went to issue the command to the three soldiers sitting or lying under the small belt of trees nearby.

Joel replaced his binoculars into their case on the saddle and pulled out his drink canteen. The water, not cool but lukewarm, was nevertheless refreshing to a parched throat. Having quenched his thirst, he secured the canteen again and waited for the scout to draw rein beside him.

In a cloud of dust, the solider, Bertram, slowed his sweating horse. 'Sir.'

'Well, Bertram? What's out there?' Joel slipped his pencil and paper from his front pocket.

'Over the other side of the valley there's a small Boer camp. Ten men. Fourteen horses.'

'Fourteen?' Joel looked up from his jotting. 'Four pack horses or do you think there could be four men you didn't see?'

'I couldn't tell if they were pack horses, they were all unsaddled. There's a river south of the camp. Extra men could've been there.'

'But you can't confirm?'

'No, Sir. Sorry, Sir.'

'Damn!' Joel glanced back at the valley slope. 'Anything else? Did the camp look fresh or a permanent?'

'Fresh. No fire that I could see.'

'Were you seen?'

'Don't think so, Sir.'

'You rode too hard down that slope. One slip and you could have been thrown or your horse made lame. I can't afford mistakes.'

Bertram flushed and lowered his eyes. 'My apologies, Sir. It won't happen again.'

Haversham came to stand next to Fidget. 'The men are ready, Sir.'

Joel nodded, then eased a map out of his pocket. 'Drink Bertram.'

The scout quickly complied, drinking so fast from his canteen that the water trickled down his chin.

Scanning his map, Joel leant down to Haversham. 'Our orders are to ascertain the Boer activity between here and here.' He pointed to the spots on the map for Haversham to see. 'Also, our instructions were not to engage the enemy unless forced to do so. We are to gather information, but not let the Boers know of our presence. Some of our forces are camped along the Orange River, we cannot have their mission jeopardised in any way.'

'Yes, Sir.'

Joel looked at his men. With Bertram back they swelled to six. They were an hour's ride from company headquarters for this region. He couldn't risk them being detected, yet his mind fought its own battle. Ten Boers against his six men.

'We would have the surprise element, Sir,' Haversham murmured, as if reading Joel's thoughts.

'Yes...'

The noon sun blistered the landscape. September. Spring in southern Africa, but where he was stationed the climate hardly changed from one season to the other and he was tired of it. For a moment, Joel longed for the coolness of a snowy winter day, not just any winter's day, but one of those they got at home. A Yorkshire blizzard, with snow drifts six foot high. He'd have a snowball fight with Charlie, Annabella and Eden. His heart expanded as always when he thought of Eden. She was lost to him and he had no one to blame but himself and the social rules of his birthright.

'Sir?'

Joel shook himself and glanced at Haversham as Fidget tossed his head and pawed the ground. 'We'll return to headquarters.'

Haversham hesitated. 'The Boer party?'

'They live to fight another day,' Joel muttered. He gave the lieutenant a wry smile. 'We're scouts, not a fighting unit. If there was a skirmish and we let just one Boer escape he could alert others to our presence. I cannot let that happen.'

'So, we ride away from the enemy.' Haversham sighed with disappointment.

'Yes, we ride away, and we live a bit longer.'

'It doesn't seem right not to challenge them, Sir.'

'Haversham, I've done more than enough of fighting in the last two years. I do not go seek it if I can help it now. I just want to live out this wretched war so I can go home to my family.'

'Yes, of course, Sir.' The young lieutenant sighed and mounted up.

Joel gathered the reins and turned Fidget about. Suddenly he wanted the quiet confines of his tent where he could write a letter to his father and one to Charlie. He'd had enough of ordering young men to their deaths, of seeing devastation, of listening to commanders who had absolutely no idea of how to run a war.

As Fidget trotted over the plain, Joel thought of his last letter from home, one that had included the details of Annabella's wedding. They even sent him a piece of wedding cake in a tin. It'd been a blow to miss his darling sister's wedding. He missed and ached to see them but yet was also frightened of returning home. What changes would have occurred in the years he's been away? Sometimes he couldn't remember their faces and would panic, then at other times their features were so clear he nearly sobbed with heartache at not being with them.

'Sir!' Haversham yelled, jerking Joel out of his reverie.

Joel wrenched around and then followed the lieutenant's pointing finger. Boers had appeared out of nowhere and galloped towards them. 'Shit!'

'Will we fight, Sir?' Haversham called, his eyes wide in a dusty face.

'We're outnumbered. We'll retreat and hope they don't catch us.' Joel heeled Fidget into a gallop.

~ ~ ~

In the misty rain Nathan circled the loaded wagon, checking the tightness of the ropes holding the cargo and then glancing down at his list. All seemed in order. He nodded to the driver. 'Right, John, off you go.'

John flicked the horses' reins and, straining, they pulled the wagon away under the arch, which supported the large wooden gates, and out of the mill yard. Nathan scanned the area, his particular domain, looking for anyone slacking off or doing something wrong, but the foul weather kept most of the workers from lingering out in the open, except for those meant to be there. For a minute he watched young Tommy Backhouse, the boy he'd set on last week. The lad showed promise. He didn't shrug off his duties or skip off down to the river whenever he thought he wasn't being observed like some of the lads did.

Nathan turned to the wagon just arrived, piled high with cotton bales all the way from America. He jumped up onto the loading platform that was level to the back of the wagon and, with a nod to the driver, took the offered paperwork from him. 'Had no problems, Jim?'

'Nay, Nathan, it all went fine.' The old driver pulled a pipe from his pocket, but on seeing Nathan's freezing glare, slid it back away. 'Sorry, gaffer, habit like.'

'Aye.' Nathan frowned at the older man's tactless disrespect towards the fire hazards that could send a flammable mill up in flames. He glanced over at Seth who walked out of the huge storage building behind. 'Get the boys to unload this, will you?'

'Want me to check it off?' Seth, his hair the colour of straw, had a cheeky smile and was a ladies' man, but for all that, he worked hard, and Nathan heavily relied on him.

'Aye, if you could.' Nathan read the paperwork. 'I've got to check the order for Rogers before it goes out.'

'Ayup,' Seth tipped his head towards the arch, 'looks like we've a visitor.'

Nathan looked up and stilled as Clifton rode through the gates. 'What the hell is he doing here?'

'Inspecting his hoped-for inheritance.' Seth laughed.

He glanced back at Seth. 'Is Collins about?' He prayed that the mill's main manager was in his office.

'Ahh, Harris.' Clifton rode up and dismounted beside the platform.

Praying for patience, Nathan jumped down. 'Are you looking for Collins?'

'Is he in charge?'

'Overall, yes. Each area of the mill has its own manager.'

'And what do you do?' Clifton's eyes narrowed.

Nathan didn't let his gaze waver. 'I'm the yard manager.'

'You like the job?'

'It'll do for me.'

Clifton tapped his riding crop against his knee-length boot. He stared at the men unloading above. 'I just came from your cottage.'

Nathan jerked. The bastard had been to his home?

'But then it isn't your cottage is it?' Clifton continued. 'It's your grandfather-in-law's isn't it?'

'What of it?'

Shrugging, Clifton flexed the riding crop between his hands. 'You don't have much, do you? Nothing that actually belongs to you, I mean.'

'What shite are you talking man?'

A malicious grin twitched Clifton's mouth. 'The cottage isn't yours, your wife was never solely yours-' He sprang back as Nathan went to grab him. From the platform above, the loading men paused to watch the scene below. 'I'd advise you against laying one finger on me. I wouldn't hesitate to contact the law.'

A raw anger pressed on Nathan's brain. He would like nothing more than to kill the bastard standing before him. 'Stay away from my family.'

'Your family?' Clifton chuckled. 'Really, you are prone to exaggeration, Harris. One daughter doesn't make a family.'

'You don't know what you're talking about.'

'I do as it happens. Just had an interesting discussion with the delightful Eden.'

Nathan clenched his hands. 'Stay away from Eden.'

Clifton inspected the tip of his riding crop. 'Impossible, dear fellow. We have many things to arrange.'

The noise of the yard seemed to drown Nathan's senses. Everything became loud, the strike of a hammer, the clip clop of the horses hooves on the cobbles, the yelling of orders, even the rain became faster, louder. What was the bastard going on about? 'You have nothing to say to Eden.'

'Wrong.' Clifton's smile returned. 'My *daughter* is high on my list of priorities. I have much to make up for.'

Nathan blinked, then the meaning of his words dawned. Josephine. With a roar of rage, Nathan sprang and grabbed Clifton by his jacket lapels. He spun and thrust the bastard against the platform. A blaze of red mist smothered everything but his intention to kill Clifton with his own hands.

'Nathan! No!' Seth and the other men jumped down and were trying to prise him off Clifton before damage was done.

'Leave go of me you madman!' Clifton yelled, his hands flaying the riding crop on Nathan's head. 'Get him off me!'

Releasing his jacket, Nathan quickly gripped both hands around Clifton's thick neck and squeezed.

'No, Nathan. For God's sake man!' Seth wrapped his arms around Nathan's shoulders, trying to break his hold. 'Let him go or yer'll be in a cell,' he whispered into Nathan's ear. 'Think, man, think. Eden, the girls. Yer can't protect them from a cell.'

Clifton's eyes bulged, his face turning a reddy-purple colour. The flaying stopped as he wheezed for air.

'Let go, Nathan.' Seth urged. 'Come on, man.'

Slowly, Nathan slackened his grip. Common sense wormed through his madness. He wouldn't go to prison for this piece of filth. He stepped back, lifting his hands free from Clifton, he felt soiled just by touching him.

Slumping to his knees, Clifton rubbed his neck, gasping for air. 'You...'

The other men, now the drama was over, flitted away, eager to get back to their work and removed from any blame. Seth touched Nathan's shoulder before he too, jumped back on the platform.

'Wait!' Clifton staggered to his feet. His eyes searched wildly about him, red welts rising on his neck. 'You...all...witnesses...'

Nathan straightened, pushed his shoulders back and lifted his head to glare at the pathetic figure. 'You're not going to the authorities and neither are you coming near my family again. Understand?'

Clifton bent over as though to catch his breath but then came up surprisingly fast and with his full force whipped the riding crop across Nathan's face.

Nathan reeled, pain biting his cheek.

'You dare tell me what to do,' Clifton screamed hoarsely. 'I'll see you dead first!' He turned to point at the men gathered. 'You all saw what he did to me. I'll call you all as witnesses.'

Seth stepped forward to the edge of the platform. 'I saw nowt, Mr Clifton, nowt at all.' He stared at his fellow workmen. 'Did any of yer see what anything?' The negative murmur rumbled around the yard and died away. The only sound was the rain dripping from the eves.

Clifton swore, hatred clear in his eyes. 'You'll all pay for this!' He strode to his horse and after two attempts managed to mount it. In the saddle, he gave them a sweeping glare, before pausing to stare at Nathan. 'This isn't the finish of it. You, Harris, have made a dreadful mistake and an enemy of me.'

'I don't want trouble, Clifton. I just want you to stay away from my family.'

'You're living on borrowed time, Harris. You'll never know a peaceful day again, I'll make certain of it.' With that, Clifton jerked the horse about and dug his heels into its flanks so that it trotted sharply out beneath the arch.

Seth jumped down to stand beside Nathan and slap him on the back. 'Bloody hell, Nath.'

Nathan held out his hand. 'Thank you. I owe you.'

'Nay, I'd not worry about that, yer've got him to think of. He'll not forget today.'

'No...'

'What the hell was he talkin' about? His daughter? What's it to do with yer?'

Nathan grimaced, amazed and alarmed at what had happened. 'It's all changing, Seth, and I don't know how to stop it...'

Later, as the rain eased and darkness stole across the wood, Nathan paused on the cottage's doorstep, his hand hovered over the latch. The lantern over the door, left there by Eden to light his way home, cast a weak glow. Only nothing felt the same. He was fast getting out of his depth and fear clutched at his chest. He didn't seek violence like other men, he hated it. Even as a little boy, a youth, he'd never been in a fight. His father had called him weak because he preferred books to boxing, but aggression had never been the answer for him, and that had totally puzzled his father. However, the mere mention of Clifton's name sent the blood pulsing in his brain and the sight of him sent common sense flying. The man should be shot, like they do to dogs gone mad.

'Nathan.'

He jumped as the voice came out of the night. Eden carrying an armful of logs stepped along the path that led from around the side of the house. He watched her hesitate, the dim brassy light etched her face in shadows, but it showed the strain on her face. She stopped and gazed at him, her eyes filling with tears. He wished that he too could cry out his wretchedness.

'You know,' she whispered.

'Aye, I got a visit.'

Her bottom lip trembled. 'He won't win, not this time.'

'No.'

A lone tear trickled down her cheek, the lamplight colouring it golden. He held out his arms and she dropped the logs and ran to him, crushing him in her hold. Kissing her hair, he murmured that everything would be all right, but they both knew the odds were against them.

Chapter 6

'Eden!'

She jumped at the harsh snap of her name and stared at Charlie. 'What is it?'

'I've been talking for two minutes and you've not listened to a word,' he accused, frowning.

'I'm sorry.' Eden stepped away from the library window, her heart heavy. She tried to be light and gay for Charlie, but her worries refused to sleep even for a moment.

'What holds your attention so acutely?' He replaced a book onto the shelf and took another.

She forced a smile. 'Nothing at all,' she lied. She couldn't tell him that with every chance she got she looked out for Clifton, wanting to know where he was at all times so she could avoid him. Two weeks. Two weeks of living in a state of nervous tension, waiting for Clifton to strike again. Each night she, Nathan and Grandfather had discussed the situation, throwing out ideas and possible plans should the worst happen, and Clifton go to the courts. She feared that Clifton would also want retribution over Nathan's aggression, and waited for something to happen. Clifton wouldn't forgive or forget and somehow, he'd want revenge on them both.

'You've lost weight.' Charlie peered at her. 'Your clothes hang off your shoulders.'

Eden sat on the deep leather chair at right angles to the fireplace. Its heat didn't penetrate the coldness she felt inside. She plucked at the grey skirt and blue blouse she wore. They weren't her best clothes, but still good, and since she wasn't a member of the family, she didn't have to wear black every day for the Colonel, though in her pocket she had a black-edged handkerchief.

Charlie came and eased into the chair opposite. The day was miserable after a week of late summer weather, which had seen him up and about and attending to the estate's affairs, but now he was confined to the house once more. 'For the last two weeks you've hardly been near the Hall and today you've come but you seem very distant. Have I done something to upset you?'

'No, of course not.' Unable to sit still, she rose and went to the book-lined wall. She pretended to study the spines, but the authors and titles held no interest. 'Shall we play cards?'

'Not in the mood today.'

She moved down the room to a gilt-framed painting of a Bradbury stud horse, a hunter of great pedigree. 'Let us write to Annabella. We'll take it in turn, a page each, she'll laugh at that.'

'Later perhaps. Come sit down. You're prowling like a caged lion.' Charlie's impatient tone made her return to the chair where she stared into the fire. He reached over and took her hands, his hazel eyes softening. 'Talk to me Eden. What is troubling you? You've dark shadows under your eyes.'

'Nothing.'

'Are the girls well? Your Grandfather or Nathan?' He tilted his head in question. 'Don't fob me off. I know you too well.'

Eden took a deep breath. 'Nathan had words with Clifton at the mill.'

'And you've been worrying about the repercussions of it?' Charlie dropped her hands to sit back and cross one leg over the other. 'You know nothing would happen to Nathan's position at the mill. He is valued and trusted.'

'Thank you.'

'Why did it happen?'

'Clifton has a way of getting under people's skin.'

'True. It mustn't have been too serious, as Clifton hasn't mentioned it to me. Please put it from your mind.'

'He hasn't mentioned Nathan, or me, at all to you in any way?'

'None at all.'

She sagged in relief. If Clifton was going to the courts, making a public show of his accusations then surely, he'd have to let Charlie know, prepare him for the family's name being mentioned.

'There's more to it, isn't there?' Suddenly, Charlie sat straighter, his expression quizzical. 'Your face has given you away, Eden. I am deeply hurt that you feel you cannot confide in me. I thought we were near brother and sister.'

'Charlie, I-I-'

'Is it about Josephine?'

She felt the warmth leave her face. 'What do you know?'

'I have believed for some time that she is not Nathan's child.'

Eden gripped the chair's arms and bowed her head. Shame filled her, shame, pain and fear. 'I thought you didn't know…'

'I'm sorry.' He was on his knees before her, lifting her face up like he'd done many times when they were children. His hands cupped her cheeks. 'I could thrash Joel for doing this to you. He should never have gone away. What does class matter? You loved each other. Everyone knew it. Father had no right to make him go, to join the army. He is the eldest son, what if he's killed? I am no use as an heir. I know Nathan loves you, has always loved you, and it was heroic of him to marry you, but-'

'Stop. Stop, Charlie!' She pulled away from him, away from his words that washed over her like icy water, dousing her in misery. She jerked to her feet and moved to the fire as thunder rolled outside. 'You have it all wrong,' her voice didn't sound her own and seemed to come from a distance.

'How do I have it wrong?'

The door was flung open and Clifton marched in, rubbing his hands. 'By Christ, it's horrid out there.' He stopped short on seeing Charlie scrambling up off his knees and his eyes widened at Eden. 'What have we here?'

'Nothing. I dropped something.' Charlie sat back in the chair and opened the newspaper that lay on the small occasional table beside him.

'How delightful to see you Mrs Harris.' Clifton smirked. 'Your absence in the last couple of weeks has been noticed.'

She tensed and inched towards the door.

'Are you attending the harvest festival tomorrow?' He sat in the chair Eden had vacated and not caring to wait for her answer turned away. 'Charlie, old fellow, we must put in an appearance at Home farm. The staff have gone to great lengths in getting it spruced up. They want us to stop by after church. I said we would.'

Charlie nodded as again thunder rumbled. 'Yes, I will try to, but the good weather of last week has disappeared again. I can't tempt fate and catch a chill. Mellors already watches over me like a mother.'

'I heard Richardson's farm is up for sale.' Clifton's eyes glowed with good humour. 'We should buy it, annex it to the estate.'

'Really?' Charlie, all interest, let the newspaper lay on his lap untouched. 'Are you certain? The Richardson family has been farming that land since before my father was born. Their land is a rare treasure we Bradburys have admired from afar.'

'From what I heard, the old man is eager to go to Canada or somewhere as primitive.' Clifton shuddered, as though the idea was something abhorrent.

'Canada? How intriguing.' Charlie frowned in thought. 'I wonder what he wants for it.'

'What does it matter? Just buy it. I know our family has yearned for the place for years. Now we have the chance to grab it.' He looked up at Eden and grinned. 'Ring for tea, will you?'

Eden stared at him, hatred narrowing her eyes. As if she would willingly do anything for him! How he could sit there and pretend everything was good between them made her sick. She could barely bring herself to speak such was her anger. She turned to Charlie and kissed his cheek. 'I'm going home. I don't want to be caught in the storm.'

He took her hand and squeezed. 'We'll talk again soon.'

She strode from the room, head held high, though she felt Clifton's eyes watch her every move.

~ ~ ~

Insistent rain thumped on the cottage's shingle roof. Great sheets of it blocked the wood from view. Eden pretended her home was isolated from the rest of the world and it brought a small measure of comfort to her. If only it was true…

'Mam, I've slipped a stitch.' Josephine held up her knitting.

Grandfather leaned over and took it from her. 'Here, darlin', let me look.'

Eden watched the pair, her grandfather's silver head bowed close to Josephine's dark one. As her habit, Eden searched her daughter's features for signs of Clifton, but as yet Josephine didn't seem to share any. Many people said she took after Eden's own mother who had been dark haired and petite and for that Eden was thankful.

'Mam,' Lillie came to lean against Eden's chair, 'can we go to the festival? Jilly Morecambe said, that after the church service, they'll have apple-bobbing and toffee and stalls.'

Stroking her daughter's burnished hair, so like her own, Eden smiled. 'If the rain lets up, we'll go, but not otherwise. I have no fancy to be out in that weather. '

'I'm tired of the rain.' Lillie sighed. 'It spoils everything.'

Grandfather laughed. 'No point in crying over something you can't alter, lass.'

Eden, her own knitting idle on her lap, watched the flames licking the logs. 'I heard that Richardson is selling up.'

'Richardson? Tommy Richardson?' Grandfather scowled.

'Yes, he's going to Canada.'

66

'Never!' He frowned. 'You sure? Nay, it can't be true, I'd have known otherwise. I only saw Tommy last week, and nowt were mentioned. Who told you?'

'I heard it at the Hall.' She couldn't bring herself to say Clifton. 'Charlie will buy it if he can.'

'Unbelievable.' Shocked Grandfather sat back in his chair, sadness clouding his blue eyes. 'I've known the Richardsons all my life. It don't seem right. Canada? Nay, I'll not believe it.'

'There's nothing wrong with wanting to start a new life or try something different.'

'Not Tommy. He's got no reason to go to a new country and start again. He must be over sixty and he's got a good son in Ned and even two grandsons. They make a tidy sum each year. Why would he want to sell a perfectly good farm?'

Eden rubbed a hand over her tired eyes. 'I don't know, Grandfather. It's just what I heard.'

'Aye, well if it's true then something stinks about it.'

She whipped her head around to stare at him. 'Something underhand?'

Grandfather nodded, his face set. 'Aye. I'll stake my life on it.'

Eden closed her eyes. Clifton. He had brought the news, seemed very excited about it…

The door opened and Nathan walked in, shaking the rain from his coat and hat.

'Had a good pint, lad?' Grandfather asked.

'Not bad.' Nathan hung up his wet outer clothes on a hook by the door and then pulled off his boots.

Grandfather leaned forward. 'Heard owt about Tommy Richardson selling up?'

'Aye. There's talk of nowt else.'

Grandfather flopped back. 'I don't believe it.'

67

Nathan squeezed Eden's shoulder, kissed the top of Lillie's head but when he went to do the same to Josephine, he hesitated for a fraction before simply ruffling her hair. 'I'm off to bed.' He left them and climbed the ladder to the loft rooms above.

A cold band circled Eden's heart. Had she imagined his hesitation towards Josephine? She must have, for Nathan had no favourite between the girls. Yet the nagging ache of pain tugged at her and she put her knitting to one side and followed him.

Nathan was pulling off his trousers and then his shirt as Eden left the ladder and walked across the confined space. For the first time in their married life she felt awkward and uncertain with him.

As Nathan tossed back the blankets and climbed into bed, he sent her a cool look. 'What?'

She swallowed. 'Just then, down below, with Josephine... You were... You didn't kiss her as you did Lillie.'

He adjusted his pillow. 'She wasn't close enough. Did you want me to trample over Grandfather's legs merely to give her a kiss?'

His disinterested tone filled her with unease. 'I just don't want you treating her differently, that's all.'

'When have I ever done that?'

Flustered, she threaded her fingers together. 'Yes, I know you haven't. Forgive me, but with the going ons with Clifton, I don't-'

'Eden I'm tired and I want to sleep.'

'It's not her fault,' she whispered, hating the distance she felt was creeping between them. Nathan had changed in the past few weeks. He hardly spoke, rarely ate with the family anymore and spent more and more of his time in the Gargrave pubs. She wanted to talk with him about Charlie believing Joel was Josephine's father, but she remained silent. Nathan had always been a little jealous of her relationship with Joel. He knew how much she had cared for Joel, had girlish dreams of them being together one day.

'I've never behaved towards her as if it was. Now can I go to sleep?'

'Nathan…' Emotion welled.

'Stop, Eden.' His face twisted as though he was in agony. 'Don't ask me to do more, please. I'm doing the best I can, *all* I can.'

'I know-'

'Then leave it.

A tear slipped down her cheek. 'I can put up with anything as long as I have you beside me.'

'I am and I always will be.' He sighed and then held out his arms and she rushed onto the bed for him to hold her tight. 'I've loved you since we were kids in school and you were Eden Morley, the lass with brains.'

'I never knew it went that far back.' She smiled into his shoulder and huddled closer, feeling safe when he spoke of his love, of the old times before Clifton, before the responsibilities of adulthood descended.

'No, you never knew that I watched you. I used to walk home behind you, even though I lived in the opposite direction from here. I used to fish the river on weekends hoping to see you or hear your laughter floating through the woods.'

'And I'd wave in greeting when I saw you walking through the wood.' She ran her fingers over his bare chest. 'You were the gloomy boy who read a lot.'

A small laugh rumbled in his chest. 'Aye.'

'We'll be all right, won't we?'

Shrugging, he fiddled with her hair. 'I don't know. I wish I did.'

'I brought this upon us,' she murmured.

'You didn't ask him to attack you.'

'No, but I could have been more…more sympathetic towards Clifton as we were growing up. Joel and Charlie cast a long shadow and Clifton had no hope of being their equal.'

'A man should learn to accept his limitations, Eden, not turn evil with jealousy and then want to hurt others.'

'We used to laugh at his attempts of being athletic and it just made him worse. We also used to cringe at his nastiness, his abuse of the Hall staff, the animals…'

'And you paid the biggest price of them all.' Nathan played with her fingers. 'The man deserves no consideration, no compassion. If he sees your weakness, he will use it against you, of that we are certain.'

'I will kill him before I'd let Josephine go with him, court or no court.'

'Forget him for now. We'll take the girls to the village, enjoy the harvest festival and think about Clifton another day.'

The following day threatened rain, but the heavy purple-black clouds held their burden while the community gave thanks in the church and then lingered along the village main street to visit the stalls selling food and bright trinkets.

After crossing the river bridge once more, Eden and the girls strolled beside the surging river towards High Green in search of Nathan and Grandfather. On the green a party atmosphere ruled. A juggler, his face painted, threw coloured balls high, a man cooked potatoes in glowing coals and an impromptu band of musicians sang lustily after being well-oiled with ale from the local landlord.

Eden sauntered across the grass, frequently stopping to talk to local families while keeping an eye on the girls, who skipped ahead, sucking their toffee. She spied old Tommy Richardson breaking away from Grandfather and hurried over. 'Grandfather?'

He watched his friend plod away, his expression sad. 'There goes a broken man, lass.'

Eden stared after Tommy Richardson. 'Why? What's happened?'

'I'm not sure, but he's aged ten years in a week. Something's not right.' Grandfather gave a knowing sniff. 'He don't look like a man eager to be off to the other side of the ocean and he wouldn't answer any of me questions.'

'I don't understand it.'

'Aye, and neither do I, but unless Tommy mentions owt, then we all have to wonder.'

She tucked her hand through his arm and walked slowly across the grass to where the girls stood laughing at a puppet show. Despite the promise of bad weather, the locals didn't want to miss the opportunity to enjoy themselves and the crowd swelled. Nathan spotted them and made his way over, he too stopping to chat with different families. Ale being sold from kegs on a cart drew Grandfather away just as Nathan made it to her side. Music filled the air and with a grin Nathan swirled her into the open.

'What are you doing?' Eden near squeaked, amazed that her quiet husband would perform such a flamboyant act before the whole village.

'I'm dancing with my wife.' He grinned.

'Have you been drinking?'

He dipped her low, completely out of step to the tune. 'Perhaps the odd ale or two.'

Laughing, Eden let him twirl and step her across the grass. Other couples, intent on making the most of their day off from work, joined in and soon the green was a bobbing mass of people. The girls catching sight of them, raced up to hug their arms about Eden and Nathan.

'We want to dance too!' Josephine clapped.

'And so you shall.' Nathan bowed formally to her and swooped her up and waltzed away, leaving Eden and Lillie to hold hands and skip about.

Eden turned, laughing with Lillie, and caught sight of Clifton talking to Tommy Richardson. Her smile slipped as Tommy grew red in the face, his shoulders sagging. Clifton grabbed the other man's arm and peered in close, their words drowned by the music and people, but Eden didn't need to hear Clifton's words, his heated gestures spoke a language of their own. She had her answers about Richardson's farm sale. At that moment Clifton looked up and spotted her. With an evil grin, he pushed Richardson away and walked towards her.

AnneMarie Brear

Chapter 7

Eden stepped in front of Lillie, ready for Clifton as he approached. Nathan and Josephine were lost in the crowd.

'Care to dance, Eden. It has been many years since we last did it.' He smiled, bowing low.

Remembering the one time they had danced, at a dinner party held at the Hall, she grimaced. Clifton had caught her on the landing and had been courteous and polite asking her to dance as the music drifted up from the rooms below. Taking pity on him and hoping he would change his ways with a little kindness she agreed. However, as the dance continued, his hand strayed from her waist to her bottom and pinched it, while in her ear he whispered obscenities. She shivered at the memory and lifted her chin. 'I'd rather kiss a toad.'

He laughed and peeked behind her. 'Who is this delightful creature we have here?'

Hiding Lillie even more, Eden glared. 'My daughter Lillie, so stay away,' she snarled, silently daring him to reach out and touch her for she'd have great pleasure in scratching his eyes out.

Clifton straightened, aware there were onlookers close by.

'Leave us alone, Clifton. We mean nothing to you.'

73

'No, you don't, but still, I am able to have a little fun.' His eyes gleamed with an inner knowledge.

'Why must you hurt people?' she whispered. 'I know of your harassment of Richardson. Was getting his farm so important to you?'

He looked startled for a moment but then shrugged. 'It is a valuable property, too good for the likes of him and his slow-witted family.'

'But it was *their* home. You believe buying this land it will make Charlie think more highly of you, instead of pitying you.'

He thrust out a hand and gripped her wrist painfully, bringing her against him. 'Stay out of business that is no concern of yours.'

'I will if you stay away from Josephine. You want to play games then I will too.' Behind her Lillie whimpered.

'Don't try to better me, bitch.' His face inched closer. 'If you do, I'll make your life a living misery.'

'Try your worst! You can do no more to me then you already have.' She wrenched her wrist free and turned away, pulling Lillie along with her.

'Mam?' Lillie gazed wide-eyed at her as they hurriedly twisted between people in search of Nathan. 'Who was that?'

'It's all right, my pet. It was no one. A silly man who'd drunk too much.' She forced herself to smile and slow down. 'Oh look, there's your Da and sister.' Breaking free of the dancers, Eden headed for the ale cart where her family stood talking and laughing with friends.

Nathan on seeing them grinned and curled Eden into his side with one hand while raising his ale to his lips. 'We're having a rest. Josephine would have me feet bleeding if we kept on.'

'I lost me ribbon, Mam.' Josephine pouted. 'But Grandfather says he'll buy me another.' She kissed Grandfather's cheek. 'Can I get a red one this time?'

'We'll see. Now, I think it's time to go home.' Eden smiled over the protesting girls' heads, though her face felt stiff from the effort. Her stomach was still knotted after the confrontation with Clifton.

'My legs are tired. Can we ask Mr Earnshaw for a lift?' Lillie sighed against Nathan's legs. 'He's given me and Josephine a lift home from school before.'

Nathan swung her up into his arms. 'Nay, my lass, I think Mr Earnshaw has retired his pony for the day.' He indicated to where the butcher swayed drunkenly against the end of the cart. 'Come on, let's be having you.' He tickled her tummy and set off.

'You not coming home with us then, Grandfather?' Eden raised an eyebrow at him.

'Nay, lass.' He raised his cup of ale. 'I'll stop on a bit here.'

'Right, well if it gets too late beg a bed with someone.' She kissed his cheek and followed Nathan and the girls.

The light started to fade and the ominous dark clouds that threatened rain all day seemed to lower even more. They sang together as they left the village and headed south over the fields and common, keeping parallel to the raging river. Its swollen contents flowing swiftly due to the recent rain, dashed against the banks and filled the air with rumbling noise unlike that of thunder.

'I'm thirsty.' Lillie yawned in Nathan's arms. 'Can we get a drink from the river?'

'No, it's not safe at the minute. It's flowing too fast.' Nathan dropped her to her feet. 'You'll have to wait until we get home and we'll have to be quick. It looks ready to bucket down.'

A fat drop of rain landed on Eden's nose. 'Bother! We won't make it. It's starting to rain.'

They rushed under the shelter of trees that lined the bank as a loud clap of thunder pounded overhead. The girls squealed, covering their ears.

Nathan frowned. 'We're going to get wet,' he yelled over the rush of the river behind them.

'Thankfully, we don't have much further to go.' Pulling the girls close, for the temperature had dropped, Eden nodded to Nathan and they continued walking, but quietly now. Yawns and shivers had replaced the singing and laughter as they trudged through the long grass on top of the bank in the grey light.

Lightening forked across the sky and at the same time the first deluge of rain hit them. Its coldness made them shiver even more and Eden worried about the girls or Nathan catching a chill. Ahead the wood loomed through the clouds and she sighed with relief. Not long now and they would be in the warmth of the cottage.

Out of the corner of her eye, Eden caught sight of movement. She paused in her step and turned just as Clifton yanked his horse to a sliding halt a few feet away. His approach had been silenced by the roar of the water. 'What are you doing here?' She snapped, wiping the rain from her face. 'Go away!'

Nathan spun around, his eyes widening. 'Clifton!' He dragged Josephine behind him, putting distance between her and the fiend on the horse.

Clifton dug his heels into the horse's flanks, urging it closer to Nathan. 'I'm not here to cause trouble, Harris. I just want to have a look at my daughter.'

Eden didn't know whether she would faint or scream with fury. Her anger won and she lunged for Clifton's leg, wanting to rip him from the saddle. 'Why can't you leave us alone! You'll never have her, never.'

The Colonel's spirited hunter spooked, side-stepped and threw its head, giving Clifton a job of controlling it. Eden hung on, dimly aware of Nathan behind her and Clifton using his riding crop across her shoulders.

'Let him go, Eden,' Nathan yelled, but she was past heeding him. She gripped Clifton's trousers and tried yanking him down. He kicked out at her, but his actions scared the horse and it plunged forward towards Nathan and the girls. With one swoop of his arm, Nathan knocked Eden away from the horse and she landed with a thump on the wet grass. The girls scurried across to her, crying, the rain plastering their hair flat on their heads.

She held them close, watching as Nathan battled Clifton. The horse reared when Nathan tried to grab the reins, unseating Clifton and with a bone-jarring crack landed on the ground and laid still.

'Oh good lord.' Eden scrambled on her knees over to him. 'Is he dead?' she cried at Nathan.

Nathan knelt beside her. 'Has he hit his head?' As he reached out to touch him Clifton sprang up and grabbed him by the throat. The force of their struggle sent them both backwards. Eden screamed with the girls joining in. Rain blurred Eden's vision as the two men wrestled furiously. Her senses recoiled at the violence, the grunts and swearing, the girls crying, the roar of the river and the non-stop rain pounding on her head. She wanted to get up, to protest, to stop them fighting, but the weight of her wet skirts kept her down, her spirit struggling in a battle of its own.

'Mam!' Josephine clung to Eden's arm with Lillie sobbing on the other side, but Eden couldn't think, couldn't act, as Nathan punched Clifton on the chin before Clifton sprang back and knocked him against a tree with a groan. On and on they went, and suddenly Eden was aware of how close they were to the riverbank. She struggled to her feet and faced the girls, shaking them so they'd focus on her. 'Run home. Do you hear me?'

Josephine's eyes widened even further. 'No-'

'Do it!' Eden took Lillie's cold wet hand and thrust it into Josephine's. 'Take your sister home. Get into the wood. You know the way. Get into the cottage and put the door bolt through.'

'But Mam-'

'Go!' Eden pushed them both in the back, stumbling the girls forward. 'Run!' she screamed at them.

She watched them for a moment, waiting until the shadowy wood swallowed their little bodies. The wood would protect them, they knew it as well as she did. She'd taught them every path, feature and tree.

A grunt brought her whirling back to the brawl. Clifton, on his knees swayed before Nathan, who brought back his fist and then let another blow connect with Clifton's face. The crunch of flesh on bone, made Eden retch. She staggered forward. 'Nathan…enough…'

Clifton shook his head like a wet ragged dog, squinted at her and smiled a bloody smile. Using a tree as a support, he hitched himself upright and leant there, breathing heavy.

Nathan coughed, dragging great gulps of air into his lungs. He held out a hand for Eden and she ran towards it.

'No. I'll not have it.' Clifton thrust away from the tree and made last attempt at knocking Nathan down. The momentum took both men back onto the edge of the slippery bank. The more they tried to get a better footing the more they slipped down. Nathan slid on hands and feet down into the water. He grabbed at Clifton, who lay on his stomach clasping handfuls of grass, trying to get a solid hold.

Throwing herself onto her knees, Eden reached down for Nathan, but he was sinking in the thick mud, the water lapping at him. 'Nathan!'

'Eden.' Clifton waved a free hand at her. 'Help me.'

She ignored him, moving away from where he lay, so he couldn't grab her. 'Nathan, down this way.' She called over the rage of the frothing water. The thick mud sucked at Nathan's boot. He was only knee deep but stuck fast. 'Unlace your boots, forget them.' Eden inched closer to the edge. She was aware of Clifton managing to slowly crawl up the bank, slithering and sliding with each bit of ground he covered. The rain came down in sheets, blurring the landscape, reducing visibility.

'I'm free, Eden.' Nathan looked up, triumphant, and at that moment, the blood ran cold in her body, for behind him, surging down the raging river was a large mass of flotsam; trees, bushes and logs, all tangled up like a giant bird's nest.

'Nathan!' She scrambled to her feet, pulling out her wet skirts that wrapped around her legs, tripping her. 'Nathan, get up on the bank. Quickly.' She pointed to the threat bearing down on him. 'Hurry, God, hurry.'

The fear in her voice made him turn to face the hazard, he stepped back, fell and scrambled up again, but the river knew no mercy. The menace bore down on him, bouncing from bank to bank before it struck him in the chest and then sucked him along with it. The swirling, murky water carried him away, tossing him like a cork in a barrel.

Hoisting her skirts high, Eden ran along the bank trying to keep up. Stunned that this was happening, she kept on running even though a pain in her side cramped. The woodland came to the water's edge and as she ran though it she lost sight of the river, glimpsing it only through gaps in the trees. A root nearly tripped her, but she stumbled on, nothing and no one could stop her.

She broke out of the wood at the spot where they always picnicked, a grassy area higher above the water. She bent double, gasping. Her breath hurt her lungs as though she sucked in razor sharp blades. Scanning the tumbling water, she saw nothing, but a dead bloated sheep washed up on the bank. Ahead the river curved around the woodland and out of view. Straightening, Eden grabbed up her filthy, wet skirts and carried on, the rain easing enough to make her vision clearer.

She followed the snaking river for another mile, searching the banks for Nathan. Exhausted, she plodded on, the weight of her wet clothes bowing her shoulders. When the rain stopped, the only noise was the gargling water pounding the rocks, scraping the banks and the drumming tattoo of the leaves dripping.

Ducking under a branch, that scattered raindrops down, making her shiver, she looked up and wondered how far she'd come. Three, four miles? Some insane little voice at the back of her mind said if she kept going, she'd be in Leeds before long. Eden wheezed and wiped the tiredness from her face and then paused. Beyond the trees ahead, she made out the lump of tangled flotsam that had carried Nathan away. She ran on, tripping in haste to reach the lethal concoction of trees, bushes, logs and dead animals, which seemed to be rammed into a hollowed-out bank, letting the end branches jutting out into the rapids like tendrils from Medusa.

'Nathan!' She slithered down the bank close to the knotted mess. Holding onto the twisted root of a tree, she waded into the water. 'Nathan.' The coldness of the knee high, murky brown water made her gasp. She held on tight, hand over hand, finding her way further into river. A dead calf, its head caught in the thick of the thorny bush had to be skirted, but thankfully the sheer mass of the flotsam had created a little bay. Here, the water no longer gushed, but gently lapped at her skirts. The cold caused her to shake. Drenched, she peered about, desperate to see him. Perhaps he had got free and was now, this very minute, walking back to the cottage? She glanced back at the bank, silently begging him to appear.

A rock beneath her boot moved and she went down on one knee, the freezing water at her chest. 'Oh God, please.' Regaining her balance, she held onto a log, but it dislodged itself from the rest and floated away, revealing Nathan face down with one arm curled around a branch.

'Nathan!' She lunged for him, dragging his face out of the water. 'You're all right. I have you now.' She struggled for footing in the rocky riverbed, but managed to free him from his entrapment and haul him towards the bank. Her skirts slowed her down. She tripped, but kept a firm hold of him under the arms. 'Darling, can you hear me?'

On the muddy bank, she pulled him backwards out of the water, nearly crying in the effort to lug his heavy body up clear of the water. His blue lips frightened her, and a sob caught in her throat at what her mind was telling her. With Herculean strength, she hoisted him onto the lip of the bank and fell against him, gulping air as her muscles screamed at the torment she'd put them through.

'Nathan?' She crawled up beside him and cupped his cheeks before she rolled him onto his side and thumped his back. 'Spit out the water!' He lay limp like a straw scarecrow.

Her gaze rested on his chest, begging it to move. She ripped open his jacket and shirt and placed her ear against his heart. Nothing. Swallowing denial, she put her ear to his mouth. Nothing. She shook him, but his head lolled from side to side. 'Dearest...' she whispered. 'Please.'

He couldn't be dead. She held her hands up in prayer and prayed hard to a God she didn't really believe in, but she'd do anything to keep Nathan. He had been her support for so long now, the one who loved her, cared for her better than any other.

She touched his face gently. Cold, so very cold. Softly, slowly she lifted his head up and placed it on her lap. 'I have you now, my love. Eden has you.'

The jingle of harness sprung her around. Clifton sat astride the hunter, his eyes wide and staring. A feral anger boiled in her chest, and he must have seen the hatred in her eyes for he held up a hand and shook his head. 'I didn't push him in, Eden. We both fell down the bank. It's not my fault.'

'Nothing ever is, is it, you bastard?'

He nudged the horse a step closer. 'Eden-'

'Stay away.' If she'd had a gun, she would have happily shot him. 'Don't ever, *ever*, come near me or my family again.'

'I never wanted this.'

'What did you want? Me to suffer because of your miserable childhood? Well, I'm suffering, you've got your wish.' She turned away from him and cuddled Nathan closer, closing her eyes against the receding hoof beats.

Chapter 8

Joel slumped back in the chair, the letter dangling from his limp fingers. A fly buzzed low around his head, but he ignored it. Outside the tent men talked, cooked their rations and cleaned their gear. The rumble of a wagon joined the noise, along with a dog's bark.

He glanced at the letter, noting Charlie's neat writing, which always got him admiring comments from their mother, while his own large loping hand was frowned at. For once he wished Charlie's months old letter hadn't reached him, that it had instead got lost amid the craziness of this war. Carefully, he flattened the letter out on the spindly table amongst his other Christmas correspondence and stared at it.

Nathan Harris was dead. Eden a widow. His mind screamed the words he refused to dwell on. She is free…free…

He smashed his fist onto the table. 'Christ almighty!' The table swayed on the uneven ground and water spilt from his cup. Joel fought the urge to lift it up and throw it against the tent's sides, to break up his cot, kick his trunk and rip the tent into rags. His chest heaved with suppressed rage. He didn't want to feel or think about Eden, it never did any good to do so. He'd survived seven years of not being near her, of not seeing her smile or laugh. She had never been his, though he liked to think she was. No, she'd made her choice soon after he left the estate. Within weeks she'd announced her plans to marry Harris. How clearer could she have been that he meant nothing to her? Friendship was all she felt, though he could have sworn it was more once...

Sucking in a calming breath he tried not to think of home, of her. It hurt too damn much. Ever since the telegram arrived about his father's death plaguing thoughts of going home had wormed in his mind, giving him sleepless nights and breaking his concentration during the day.

Gently, belying his inner torment, he rubbed his finger over her name in Charlie's letter. Why it bothered him so much this time, he didn't understand. Plenty of times Charlie and Annabella had written of her, mentioning her wedding, the birth of her two daughters. Only, then it had hurt for a while and he forced himself to get on with his soldiering and shield his heart from everything that concerned him in England, like his father's death. However now, now Eden was free, widowed. Alone. And he loved her. The chains of war restricted him from leaving Africa, of going home and helping her, and his frustrations grew. He was tired of fighting, tired of caring for men. He wanted to go home, to Eden. Eden had loved him once, he was sure of it...

A stirring outside the tent gave some warning of a visitor and Joel looked up as the tent flap was flung back and Frank Drury stuck his head through the gap. 'Ho, my good man!' He grinned, revealing crooked white teeth from beneath a bushy moustache. 'Care to join me for a nip or two?'

'It's barely 4 o'clock, man. The sun's not down yet.'

'So?' Frank stepped into the tent, thrusting his hands into his trouser pockets. 'You on duty tonight?'

Joel sighed. 'No, thankfully. I've done four straight.' He carefully folded his letter, hiding Charlie's words, and slipped it into his breast pocket.

'I heard you'd done another successful assignment. The rumour is you personally shot ten Boers, before the rest of their party surrendered. You need to calm down, man. You make the rest of us look bad.'

'It was five not ten.' Joel gave him a wry smile, knowing Frank's aversion to participating in real soldiering. 'I'll gladly allow you to take charge of the next one, my friend.'

'God no! What, get close enough for them to actually fire on me?' Frank sniffed in distaste. 'My role in this God forsaken place is of a more strategic position than combat, you know that.'

'Indeed, I do.'

Frank peered at Joel's small collection of books on the table. 'We just received fourteen new prisoners, women and children again.' He lifted a book up and inspected the spine. 'Bloody scandal it is. I don't want to be responsible for their wellbeing, not women or children. I hope they move them on. I can't stand to see the children stare at me as I go by.' He shivered. 'Bloody war.'

Suddenly the tent seemed too cramped, no air. Joel jerked to his feet and pushed Frank out. 'Come on then, old fellow, let us drown our sorrows. Shall we sample some of your finest brandy, or is it whiskey you've had sent from home?'

Lifted out of his doldrums, Frank grinned. 'That's the spirit. A few hours of liquid friendship soon puts the world to rights.'

As they walked across the camp towards the officer's mess, passing men tending to their fires and equipment, a voice sang clear. The whole camp seemed to quieten as the man sung the Christmas carol in a lilting, choir boy voice.

Silent night Holy night
All is calm all is bright
'Round yon virgin Mother and Child
Holy infant so tender and mild
Sleep in heavenly peace
Sleep in heavenly peace

Joel's steps faltered as the words hung in the air, reminding him of another Christmas Eve when he, Charlie, Annabella and Eden had gone sledding down the hill near the frozen river. They'd behaved like children and not like the young adults they'd become. He remembered the bitter cold of that Christmas and of Eden giving him an emerald green scarf, she'd knitted herself. A scarf that he still had, buried deep in the bottom of his trunk. How they had laughed that winter. It was all so innocent and fun. The games they played while the snow fell outside, the hours they spent in front of the fire reading and talking.

Thinking of that special Christmas made his heart grew even heavier with want, but those days were gone, never to return. That had been their last Christmas together.

'Joel?' Frank tapped his arm and frowned.

'What?' Joel blinked, realising they were at the mess. 'Sorry, I was miles away.'

'Somewhere good I hope.' Frank laughed, going inside.

Joel paused, listening to the last notes of the carol dying softly. 'I was thinking of home...' he whispered.

~ ~ ~

The howling wind battered the cottage and outside the trees creaked in protest to the thrashing they received. Eden hung up the paper chain and placed the oranges in the socks hanging from the mantelpiece.

'A wild Christmas this is, my dear.' Grandfather said, sucking his pipe.

'Yes, but no snow as yet.' She added a strip of liquorice to each sock and a square of black treacle toffee.

'Did you put the pennies in?' Grandfather pointed his pipe to the girl's bulging Christmas socks.

'Aye, in the toe bit, as a surprise.' She folded two new handkerchiefs, each with the letter J or L sewn onto the corner. Lastly, she put in skipping ropes, yellow ribbons for Lillie and red ribbons for Josephine. 'Charlie said in his note that he's bought them each a book.'

Grandfather nodded and placed another log on the fire. 'You'll go there tomorrow with the girls?'

Eden stiffened. She hadn't been to the Hall since Nathan died eight weeks ago – the longest she'd been away. 'I sent a message that I would, but I'll not be there long, an hour at most.'

'Aye, lass. Go and see Master Charlie, he's down again with that chest of his, he'll be wanting to see you.' Grandfather glanced at her. 'I've heard nothing about *him* being there.'

'No, nor I.'

'Though apparently he left shortly after Nathan drowned. With him gone and Master Charlie ill, that old windbag Mrs Fleming has been ruling the roost at the Hall as though she was master and mistress all rolled into one. Silly old trout. She'll get caught one day, when Master Joel is home.' Grandfather gave the fire another jab with the iron poker. 'Whispers have it that she's selling off small pieces of the family's silver, thieving trollop.'

'It's not the first time she lined her own pockets and I doubt it'll be the last. No one will speak of her light-fingered habits, for she scares the staff worse than the devil. She turns any girl out without references if they so much as look at her in the wrong way and I know Clifton has got more than one with child in the past and they've been let go without a farthing to help them.' Eden straightened the hanging socks, checked the nails held well into the wood. The injustice of Mrs Fleming controlling the Hall made it too difficult to fight the constant anger she'd felt since Nathan's death. What was fair about her losing Nathan, a wonderful father and husband, when the likes of Fleming and Clifton abused their positions? She took a deep breath to calm herself, but then she remembered what she heard at the market. 'I was told in the market on Saturday that the Richardsons' have gone. Clifton got his way then, like I told you he would. He will stop at nothing to get want he wants.'

'Aye, the scoundrel that he is. I can't help feeling sorry for the Richardsons', poor sods. Still, Tommy was a stubborn old bugger and wouldn't listen to reason. Clifton made him an offer he couldn't refuse.'

'Clifton made his life a misery until he signed more like.'

Grandfather shrugged. 'That too, I suppose. But I told Tommy Master Charlie wouldn't make him go through with the sale if he spoke up about Clifton's threats. Only, then with Master Charlie getting ill again, Tommy simply couldn't fight anymore, not after he sold all the stock.'

'I should have done more. I knew what Clifton was doing but then with Nathan dying…'

'Nay lass, it weren't your fault. You're not responsible for Clifton's actions.'

'No, but there's times when I think every evil thing he does is because of me in some way.' Eden collected her sewing and sat in the chair opposite Grandfather. She was sewing together knitted squares the girls had done into a blanket for winter, but her hands shook, and she had to put it down again.

'You're not eating enough, Eden. You're all skin and bones.'

'I can't eat.'

'We can't afford for you to get sick, lass. I can't look after the girls on me own. They've just lost their da, they can't lose you too.'

She frowned at him in annoyance. 'I'm not going to die!'

'You will the way you're going,' he snapped at her. 'Do you think Nathan would be pleased to see you in this state?'

'I-'

'When was the last time you washed your hair? It's the colour of dirt as it is now. I used to enjoy watching the fire bring out the gold in it when it was newly washed.'

She blinked at him in surprise, her fingers touching her hair. Nathan used to say it was the colour of ripe chestnuts…

'Heat up some water, lass.' Grandfather's eyes softened his voice gentle. 'You wash your hair for Christmas and then come by the fire here and I'll dry it for you like I used to when you were little.'

Tears simmered behind her eyes and she reached out and squeezed his gnarled hand. 'I'll pick up again, I promise. It's just been so…so dreadful.'

'I know my lass, I know.' He placed his other hand over hers. 'Let's hope the New Year brings some happiness back to us.'

She nodded and rose. 'I'll go heat the water.'

The next morning, after the girls spilled out the contents of their socks and ate fried streaky bacon and boiled eggs, Eden made them wrap up well against the cold before they left the warmth of the cottage for the frozen wood.

'Will Master Charlie have a present for us, Ma?' Josephine asked, burying her chin deep in her red scarf.

'You'll have to wait and see, and you'll not ask either. A present is to be given not begged for.' Eden watched Lillie run ahead and pick up a stick.

'I'll not ask, I was only wondering. He gave us a doll each last year. Da said…before he-he…'Josephine blinked and swallowed. 'He was thinking of getting a puppy.'

Eden's heart turned over. 'Well, we'll see.' Without Nathan's wage now, she'd be lucky to feed themselves never mind a dog. She shook the depressing thought from her mind. 'Lillie, don't get mucky.' Taking Josephine's hand, she quickened the step, eager to have the visit over with. As much as she loved Charlie, she didn't want his gentle concern today, her first Christmas without Nathan, for she was sure that one kind look from him will have her undone.

They left the dark wood, crossed the field and then the deer park, before going through the gate and stepping through the Hall's gardens. She led the girls to the side entrance she always used. Once in the corridor, she helped the girls to take off their outer clothes and hang them in the small boot room. Emerging into the corridor again, Eden paused as Mrs Fleming came out of the servants' entry to the dining room.

'I see you have invaded this house again with your unwanted presence.' Mrs Fleming sneered, her gaze flicking over the girls as though they were scum off the streets.

'As always, Mrs Fleming, your words affect me little.' She pushed the girls ahead and swept by the odious woman.

'Mr Clifton might not be home at present, but I assure you I let him know of everything that happens in this house.' Mrs Fleming fingered the bunch of keys at her waist. 'He particularly asked me to keep an eye on you and your slanderous gossip about Mr Clifton being a party to your husband's death.'

Eden turned and strode back, her anger rose threatening to choke her. 'You toad of a woman! Report back to that pig of a man as often as you like, I don't care. Clifton might have scuttled off to the hole he lives in, but the fact remains Nathan would never have been in that river if it wasn't for Clifton stopping us on the way home.' Eden leaned in closer. 'And as for telling tales, shall I go to the constable and inform him of the family's missing silver?'

Mrs Fleming's eyes widened. 'I-you!'

'Think on that, Mrs Fleming.' Eden spun back to the girls and marched them up the stairs and along to Charlie's sitting room. They met Mellors outside the door with a tray.

'Oh, Mrs Harris.' He smiled, his eyes softening even if his proud bearing didn't. 'It's a pleasure to see you here. Mister Charlie has gone on about your visit all morning.'

'Are you well, Mellors?' She lightly touched his sleeve, noticing how his hair was nearly snow-white now.

'Very. Now off you go in and I'll take this tea back downstairs and have the feast brought up that Mister Charlie ordered for your visit.' He grinned down at the girls. 'Cook's made some special treats for you both.'

Eden ushered the girls inside the sitting room, and they ran over to Charlie where he sat in front of the fire and kissed his pale cheeks.

'My girls!' He laughed. 'How I have missed you both. Your mother has been punishing me by not letting you come.'

'What tales you tell, Charlie.' She smiled and bent to kiss him too. 'If you stop pretending you're ill for a while, they'd be able to visit more often.'

'Pretending?' He laughed again at her jest. 'If only, my dear, if only.'

She patted his thin hand and then sat opposite him while he fussed over the girls, giving them their main presents and then lots of little ones. 'You've spoilt them, Charlie.'

Over their heads he gazed at her, the blue around his lips pronounced. 'No, never, dearest Eden. You and the girls are all I have at the moment.'

'No news from Annabella?'

'A cable two weeks ago. They're on their way home. She sails into England next month. They were in India when the news of father's death finally reached them.'

'I didn't know they were going to India while on their honeymoon.' Eden watched the girls settle themselves over on the window seat with their books and paper cones of sugared sweets.

'Likely Carleton wanted to find some business interests there. After all, Annabella will want to be kept in the style she is accustomed too.' He winked. Some colour was returning to his cheeks. 'Poor Carleton, being a moorland landowner won't be enough for Annabella, she'll want him to advance in his political ambitions and money is needed for that.'

'Knowing our darling Annabella, she'll want an invitation to King Edward's coronation too.'

'Her heart would burst at the thought. She was born in the wrong family, that one.' He chuckled. 'Being a Colonel's daughter wasn't enough, she should have been a princess for she adores pomp and pageantry.'

Eden smiled, thinking of her dearest friend. How she had missed in her in these last months. 'She's been gone too long, Charlie. Five months without her is too long.'

Before he could answer, Mellors returned bearing a large silver tray with two maids following him, carrying more trays laden with cold meats and cakes. Eden stared at them as they set it all out on Charlie's small table by the window. Only when they had left the room, did she mention them. 'Who are those girls, Mellors?'

'New parlour maids Mrs Harris started this week.'

'What happened to Mary and Flo?'

Mellors shifted from foot to foot and avoided her gaze. 'Well, I'm not sure...'

'Nonsense, you know what happens here.'

He sighed while pouring out the tea. 'Mary was with child and Flo started trouble,' he murmured so the girls wouldn't hear.

Eden closed her eyes. 'Trouble? What kind?'

Mellors moved away a little from Charlie and the girls who were making a racket over the culinary delights on the trays. 'You remember what Flo was like, rather loud and mouthy.'

'Yes, but loyal.'

He nodded. 'Aye well she made it known that Clifton had raped Mary. Mrs Fleming called her a liar and in front of everyone demanded for Mary to admit to lying to Flo about her attack. We all know Clifton did it, it's his style. How many maids has he gone through over the years? Oh, I know Mrs Fleming has tried to keep it quiet, but word gets around.'

'So, both Mary and Flo were sent packing?'

'Yes, and without references either. Disgrace it is. Mrs Fleming is worse than many officers I've soldiered under.'

'Do you know of her stealing too?'

'Of course, but she's always had Clifton to protect her. He turns a blind eye as long as she turns one too about his misadventures.'

'It's gone on long enough. We should tell Charlie. I can't stand by and see young girls ruined like I-' She took a step back, alarmed at how close she came to speaking of her secret. 'We cannot let it go on. Charlie needs to know.'

'No. He's ill and can stand no more burdens.' Mellors arranged the cups on the saucers into rows and shook his head. 'He should never have gone to your Nathan's funeral. That cool, damp day simply put him back in bed for weeks. But he wouldn't listen to me.'

'He needs to know-'

'What do I need to know?'

They both jumped guiltily as Charlie stood there with his hand in his pockets. Eden realised how dreadfully thin he was, as though death rode his shoulders. Suddenly she couldn't bear to lose him, not another one she loved so much. 'Why nothing at all. Mellors and I were simply going to steal some cakes here, leaving you with less-'

'What a terrible liar you are, dearest, you will never learn, will you?' A wry smile played on his lips. 'The truth if you please because your serious faces had nothing to do with cakes.'

'Sir-'

'No thank you, Mellors.' Charlie held up his hand and for a moment was every inch of his father. 'I'd like Eden to tell me.'

'Now's not the time, Charlie, the girls-'

'Are busy and not taking the slightest notice of us. Now pass me a teacup and let us sit down, for I'm sure your information isn't going to be pleasant and the tea will help to sweeten it.'

Chapter 9

'You're to be the housekeeper?' Grandfather sat forward, frowning. 'When did all this come about?'

'At Christmas.'

'Why didn't you tell me days ago, when it was first mentioned?'

'Because it was Christmas Day and you had gone to the village for an ale. It was late by the time you'd returned. Actually, I wanted a few days to think about it.'

'Are you sure you want the position?'

Eden rubbed a hand over her eyes and sighed. She had thought about nothing else since Charlie offered it to her last week. 'Yes, and as I see it, we need me to take it. Without Nathan's wage we have little money. You know I had to get permanent work'

'Aye, I know, but there?'

'I can do it.'

'I know you can do it, lass, but have you thought what it means?' He rested back in the chair and waved his pipe stem at her. 'You'll be at Clifton's beck and call.'

Eden looked at the fire, glowing red in contrast to the snow outside. She huddled in front of its warmth, but was still cold. She wondered if she'd ever feel warm again. 'Charlie has written to Clifton about the maid's accusations and Mrs Fleming's impending removal. He's been advised to not return to the Hall until he can control his…behaviour. He isn't expected for some time anyway, since Charlie gave him a good sum of money for acquiring the Richardson's place. Only Charlie is disgusted now he knows Clifton bullied them out.' She took a deep breath. 'He'll not like the letter I'm sure, but Charlie was livid when he was told about Mary being with child and how Mrs Fleming was filling her own pockets and Clifton knew about it.'

'Yes, he would have seen that as being a traitor to the family.' Grandfather tugged the blanket on his knees higher.

'Sadly, Charlie still respects the family loyalty that was drummed into him as a child. No matter what Clifton has done, Charlie won't denounce him altogether.'

'I gather you didn't tell Charlie about Josephine then?'

She shook her head. 'No, it wasn't the right time. There was enough to discuss already, and it was a sour topic for Christmas after all, plus the girls were getting tired and restless so we came home.'

'Has Mrs Fleming been told?'

'No, it is to be done in the morning. Charlie wanted to have Christmas and New Year celebrations over with. There have been a few visitors lately, now Charlie's been up and about again.'

'When will you start working?'

'Tomorrow. Charlie wants me there when he confronts Mrs Fleming.'

'There'll be hell to pay, lass. Mrs Fleming has held that job for years.'

'Yes and done well out of it too.' Eden collected their empty cups, placed them in the sink and then tidied the room a bit, suddenly needing to be active despite the late hour.

'Will you have to move into the Hall now?'

Eden paused in folding Lillie's apron. She laid it on the back of the kitchen chair and crossed to sit near the fire again. 'No. I'll come home every night.'

'But a housekeeper needs to be there in case anything happens. It's a live-in position.'

'Not this housekeeper.' She smiled ruefully. 'They know I'm not far away, if they need me. Besides, Mellors is there. I told Charlie I would only take the position if I could still come home.'

'And what happens when Clifton does come back, which he will, he always does once his money has run out.'

She held her hands out to the heat. 'I'll deal with it.'

'What of his threats about Josephine? He won't give up. Nathan's death might have scared him enough to stay quiet for a while, but he'll soon return to his old ways.'

'I'll go to Charlie. Tell him everything.' Eden listened to the wind whistle down the chimney. 'Clifton is more worried about the money he's able to get from Charlie than he is about taking Josephine from me. He knows if I tell Charlie the truth then he'll be an outcast from the family for ever.'

'The man's a coward.'

'Yes, he is, and I'm no longer frightened of him.' A hard edge came into her voice and she raised her chin. 'He can do no more to me. He'd be a fool to try. I've not told Charlie before now because he's not been strong enough to cope with it, but should Clifton's threat ever become real then, I'm sorry, but I wouldn't hesitate to burden Charlie with the knowledge his cousin raped me. I have to protect the girls at all costs, especially since we no longer have Nathan with us.'

Grandfather puffed on his pipe. 'Well, lass, play that trump card the minute Clifton gives you trouble. He deserves no pity, and Master Charlie needs to stand up to him. Master Joel would've if he'd known.'

She placed her hand on his knee, her confidence waning for a moment. 'Was I wrong not to tell everyone at the time?'

Grandfather's expression softened. 'Nay lass, we can't rake over old embers. What's done is done. We have to make the best of it. Go on up to bed. You'll have a day of it tomorrow.'

~ ~ ~

'You're jesting, surely?' Mrs Fleming's eyes widened, her mouth dropped open and she stared from Charlie to Eden and back again. 'You are joking aren't you, Master Charlie?'

'I assure you, I am not.' Charlie stood straight and imposing. His colour was good today, the odious task in telling Mrs Fleming she was dismissed had put steely glint in his hazel eyes.

Eden, standing by the door, watched them, waiting to see how the interview would play out.

'But I don't understand.' Mrs Fleming's wheedling voice was the only sound in the housekeeper's rooms opposite the kitchen. 'I've served this family for years. I've-'

'You've done well out of the bargain too, Mrs Fleming, don't bother to deny it. I am aware of your pilfering, your double standards and downright cruelty.'

Mrs Fleming's face paled to a dirty grey colour. 'If-If I have managed to upset you, sir, please allow me to apologise and put it right again. You know I would do anything for this family, anything.'

Charlie walked stiffly towards the chest of drawers on the far wall. 'I believe you have done enough, Madam. Now, if you please, open your desk drawers and cupboards.'

'What?' Mrs Fleming blinked, gaped. 'My-my drawers? Why?'

'The spoils of war, Mrs Fleming.' Charlie clasped his hands behind his back, so reminiscent of his father. 'You'll leave here with only your clothes, a reference and money I will give you. The rest stays.'

Her piggy eyes brightened like buttons with fury. 'What money is here is my own, saved from my wages over the years.'

'Show me the amount you store in this room and also any bank account you have. Now.'

Eden clenched her hands in the folds of her black skirt, hoping Mrs Fleming wouldn't make a fuss and simply go peacefully.

'You must have rocks in your head if you think I'll show you anything.' Mrs Fleming stormed towards the wardrobe and pulled down a large bag from the top. 'I'll not have you going through my private things.'

'And I'll not have you leaving this house with the profits of years of stealing.' Charlie's disdain etched his face. 'If you wish for a reference, I advise you to cooperate.'

'Go to Hell!' She opened the top drawer of the chest by the wall, grabbed an armful of clothes and stuffed them in the bag. 'Go on then, ransack the room, turn it over from top to bottom, but you'll not find a thing in here.' Her face screwed up in anger, she pushed past Charlie and emptied another drawer. 'Go on then,' she tormented. 'See what you can find. I weren't harming no one and you still had this house run well, so why bother causing a row about it now, hey?'

'I didn't know about your behaviour until recently. The scam you and my cousin have going is intolerable to me.' Charlie sagged a little and a cough rumbled in his chest.

Fleming laughed. 'Aye, spit it up lad, you'll not be long for this world.'

Eden sprang forward and slapped her pert face. 'How dare you speak to him like that.'

Shocked, her cheek reddening, Fleming glared. 'Oh, you think you're so clever don't you. I know you're behind this. You've been wanting me out for years.'

'You didn't deserve to be here. You've abused your position, brought shame to the Bradbury name.'

'Shame? Me? What I did is what every housekeeper in the country does. Ho no, missy, the only shame in this room is you. Well, I'll not keep quiet about you for another minute. I know-'

'Shut your mouth!' Eden stepped forward to grab her, but Fleming brought her fat, flabby arm back ready to floor Eden with it, only Charlie grabbed it in time and pushed Fleming away. 'Don't you raise a hand to her.'

'Huh, want to protect her, do you? She been keeping your bed warm, has she?' Fleming sneered. 'Well, that's hardly surprising is it? What else could she be doing in your room all these years? It's not as if she hasn't enjoyed other men, is it? Her poor husband was fooled time and again, Master Joel, Mr Clifton, you, I bet she even had the old master before he snuffed it too.'

'Get out, you filthy hag!' Charlie lunged only to gasp and double over. 'Never…step foot on Bradbury property again.'

'Bradbury property? That's a laugh. You on your death bed, Miss Lady Muck swanning around the continent with her weak jawed husband and the major in the firing line on a daily basis. You lot will be lucky to see the rest of the year out.' Fleming bustled over to the door, but paused and turned back. 'There's a good chance it'll be Mr Clifton's property one day and then I'll be back where I belong. Just you wait and see.' The door slammed behind her and Eden forced herself to move and comfort Charlie.

Together they stumbled out of the room and up the corridor. Charlie was coughing, and Eden shouted for Mellors, praying he was in hearing distance.

'I can't make the stairs, Eden.' Charlie whispered, sucking in air. 'Drawing room…'

'Mellors!' Eden shouted again and guided Charlie into the drawing room and onto a chair by the fire. 'Lord, we should never have let it get out of hand. I'm sorry Charlie, for my part.'

He shook his head, resting back. 'No one's fault…' He closed his eyes and smothered the coughing that shook his body the best he could.

Mellors rushed into the room, wide eyed. 'Eh, I'm that sorry Master Charlie. Jane came and got me. I didn't hear, didn't know…'

Eden straightened. 'He can't make the stairs, you'll have to get help to carry him up. Get someone to warm his bed first.'

'Aye, right away.' Mellors spun on his heel and left at a run.

Charlie waved half-heartedly at her, his eyes closed, sunken in his head. 'Eden.'

She took his hand and put it against her cheek. 'What is it?'

'Take care of everything,' he whispered.

'Of course.'

'Telegram Joel.' His Adam's apple bobbed as he swallowed. 'Tell him to come home. He'll know what to do, how to take care of it all.'

'He can't leave a war, Charlie, not even for us,' she murmured, her chest tightening. 'We'll be all right. I'm here now and will make sure all is as it should be.'

'Too much for you...'

'Nonsense.' She compelled the strength back into her tone. 'I've lived within the shadows of this house and the estate all my life, why wouldn't I be able to keep it going until Joel returns or you are stronger.'

'I'll...never be strong again.'

'Tosh. I won't hear of it. You've had a setback, but I'm in charge now, there'll be no more problems and you can concentrate on getting well again.'

'It'll be spring soon.'

She smiled. 'Yes, and warm weather. We can sit out in the garden.'

He coughed, harking up spit, which sent him scrambling for his handkerchief in his pockets.

'Here, use mine.' She had hers habitually tucked in her sleeve and thrust it at him. 'It's nowt but a bit of rag, I don't need it back.'

Charlie bent forward, covering his blue-tinged mouth, coughing and spluttering, panting for air.

Eden banged his back. 'There now, that's it. Easy, easy.'

When the spasm passed, he leaned back again and lowered the cloth from his mouth. Blood stained the white material as though it had been a bandage on an open wound. Eden put a hand to her throat.

Charlie stared at it. 'So,' he whispered, 'this is the beginning of the end.'

Chapter 10

Dust motes drifted on the sun rays shining through the open windows. Eden, hair tied up in a tight bun at her nape and wearing a large white apron over her black dress, supervised the spring cleaning of the Hall. Alive with industry, the house had been subjected to a thorough clean from attics to cellars. Curtains were taken down, washed and re-hung, floors polished, carpets beaten, painting frames cleaned, and gold leaf reapplied where necessary. Each room received the same treatment. New mattresses were bought for the beds, carpet replaced on the stairs, the contents of the cellars, valuable silverware and other priceless ornaments and articles catalogued throughout the house.

In the three months since Mrs Fleming's dismissal, Eden had found a particular fulfilment in running the house and staff. She believed the role of housekeeper suited her well and found satisfaction in coping with the large responsibility that was hers. With Charlie's complete support she hired extra maids and slowly wiped out the stain of Flemings.

Now, as March heralded spring and the gardens became green with new growth, Eden prepared for Annabella's return home. Charlie had received a telegram yesterday alerting them to her arrival sometime this week. Her dearest friend had been gone over nine months and sorely missed.

As the two parlourmaids cleaned the windows, Eden instructed the boot boy, Seth and one of the young gardeners, brought inside to help, to roll out the carpet. 'Keep it straight, Seth.' Frowning, she bent to help pull the carpet to one side.

The two footmen entered the drawing room with Mellors. 'Mrs Harris. Are you ready for the furniture to be brought back in?'

'Yes, thank you, Mellors.' She smiled at him. 'Only the sofa can be placed on the left of the fireplace this time and can you bring in one of the ferns from the conservatory, it can be placed near the window now the weather is warmer.'

'The Chippendale Pier table to go under the painting as before.'

Eden chewed her bottom lip. 'Yes, it is too big to fit anywhere else.'

While the two footmen carried the furniture back into the room, Eden left the drawing room. In the hall, she paused on hearing a carriage wheels crunching along the gravel drive. She put a hand to her forehead and tried to think who was expected today.

Mellors came to stand beside her. 'Master Charlie didn't tell me we were entertaining today.'

'Nor me.' Whipping off her apron, Eden looked to the front door. 'Whoever it is, can you take them straight up to Charlie and I'll inform Cook to set a tea tray.'

Mellors turned, but at the same time the front door was flung open and Annabella stood there, eyes wide with excitement, and looking so fashionable in a narrow grey-blue skirt and matching bodice. 'I'm home!'

'Annabella!' Eden gasped.

'Darling Eden,' she squealed, and ran into Eden's arms. They danced around the hall like children, hugging and laughing, crying and chattering like monkeys.

'I've missed you very much.' Eden held her dearest friend tight.

'And I missed you. I wish you had come with me. We would have had such fun together.'

'I doubt your husband would have approved.' Eden chuckled. 'How are you really?'

'Good. Very happy to be home, actually. I never want to leave again.'

'You have to tell me about your travels.'

'Yes, of course. I saw so many places. The people are different abroad. Oh, the heat in India! I couldn't leave there quickly enough, I promise you.' She chuckled. 'I shall tell you everything.'

'And your husband? Where is he?' Eden looked out the open door, expecting to see him.

'Oh, he's away to his precious farm and mother. You know what he's like.' Annabella waved a dismissive hand, her face screwing up with annoyance. 'I refused to go there without seeing my home first and it annoyed him. So, he has gone along without me and will return later.' Annabelle stepped back and remembered Mellors. Her smile became wistful. 'Mellors, Papa's dear loyal friend. How are you?'

'Well, Mrs Carleton.' Mellors bowed. 'Pleased to see you home.'

'It is good to be home, though strange too.' Annabella tilted her head, her large hat placed at an angle, covered her face for a moment. 'It doesn't seem right to not have Papa here to greet me. The news devastated me. It didn't seem real. It still doesn't I suppose.' She glanced around the hall. The doors were open to the drawing room showing cleaning activity. 'I feel much has changed since I went away. In many ways I wish I'd never gone.'

Eden touched her arm. 'Charlie longs to see you, dearest.'

Annabella's brilliant smile lit up her face. 'Charlie. How is he? I have presents for him, and for you too, Eden, and the girls. Mellors, do be a dear and have them brought in from the carriage.' She lifted her skirts and hurried upstairs only to turn halfway and stare down at them. 'Is he in his room?'

'Yes, though today he is feeling much better and has been working on the accounts.' Eden put her hand on the banister rail. 'He's much changed, Annabella. Don't be alarmed by his appearance.'

Her face paled and she held out her hand. 'Come with me, Eden.'

Shaking her head, Eden sighed at how little Annabella had changed despite her marriage. She still seemed such an innocent. 'You don't need me to be with you. It's Charlie, not some stranger. Now go, and I'll have some tea waiting for you in the morning room.'

'Very well.' Annabella nodded and slowly ascended the staircase.

Mellors turned for the door. 'It'll do Master Charlie some good to have her here.'

'Yes, he must be tired of our old faces.' Eden smiled and left the entrance hall and walked down to the morning room. This was the first room to be finished in the spring clean. She surveyed the polished furniture, the fresh curtains, and with a smile the vase of daffodils on the low table between the chairs. Decorated in hues of pale green and lemon this room always felt welcoming. She rang the bell pull at the side of the fireplace and when the maid arrived ordered tea for Annabella and herself.

Within moments, Annabella walked through the doorway, a frown creasing her flawless skin. 'Oh, Eden. Why didn't you tell me he was so bad?' She held a dainty white handkerchief to her nose. 'I never expected to see him so frail.'

'I did write.' Eden hugged her close. 'I sent my last letter a week ago, only you travelled around so much I was never certain they'd reach you.'

'Yes, letters were often forwarded on from one hotel to another.'

'Come sit down, tea will be here presently.'

'I didn't stay long with Charlie as I could see he was tired.' Annabella sniffed.

They sat on opposite chairs and silently regarded each other. Physically, Annabella hadn't changed much at all. Perhaps she carried a little more weight, but was still slender and beautiful. She'd removed her large hat and her tawny hair was curled up in an arrangement sprigged with tiny white rosebuds. Eden, dressed in black mourning, felt a hundred years old in comparison.

Once the tea tray arrived, Eden busied herself serving while Mellors brought in the small trunk containing the presents. With a bow he left, but at the door he indicated with a nod of his head that he'd be close by. Eden smiled at him, thankful to have such a supportive friend in the house.

'So much has happened.' Annabella sighed. 'I can't believe half of it, truly I can't. Papa gone, your dear Nathan, and Charlie so sick.'

Eden lifted the teapot and filled two teacups. 'The months you've been away have been difficult.'

'I'm so cross that we were away so long. I should have come home…'

'Why didn't you?'

Selecting a tart from the cake stand, Annabella shrugged one shoulder. 'There was so much to see and do, and Carleton was intent on bettering himself. All that investing and business. I was most put out by it. He spent more time with gentleman acquaintances than with me.' She pouted like a girl and Eden felt that old stirring of annoyance with her, which rose every once in a while.

'Do you realise how selfish you sound?'

Wide-eyed Annabella stared. 'Why? What could I have done anyway? I could never have returned home in time for Papa's funeral.'

'I know that. But you must have thought of Charlie, being here alone.'

'He has you, and Mellors.' She sipped her tea, unconcerned. 'You've always been far more sensible than me. If the truth be told, I did want to come home, but Carleton wouldn't hear of it. He refused to listen to me.'

'He wasn't sympathetic?'

'I suppose, in his own way. We were so far away, Eden, you must understand. But enough of that subject.' Annabella tossed her head. 'What is done is done. Now, let me tell you of the things I saw and did.'

'So, it seems,' Eden murmured. As much as she loved Annabella, there were times when Eden wanted to slap her silly. Sighing back her disappointment, she listened to Annabella's enthusiastic chatter. Something in her friend's manner alerted Eden to an undercurrent of unease. Annabella's edginess wasn't normal. Granted, she'd always been a bit high-strung and flighty, but her behaviour today held a brittleness that made Eden anxious.

After another ten minutes of Annabella's prattle about the heat, parties, fashion, rude servants and the boredom of ship life, Eden steered the conversation in another direction. 'What are your plans now? Will you live at Carleton's farm or has he bought you a splendid house somewhere?'

Annabella wrinkled her button nose. 'I'll not live with his mother, no thank you. You know how exhausting she is with her rules and prejudices. I'm in fear of offending her every time I see her.' She bit into the tart. 'It should be amusing really, after all, the Bradburys are far wealthier and have more social standing than the Carletons, but to listen to her you wouldn't think so.'

'That is your mother-in-law, Annabelle, you shouldn't speak—'

'Oh poo. We can't stand the sight of each other and everyone knows it.' Placing her cup and saucer back on the tray, Annabella glanced at Eden from under her lashes. 'I am actually in a bit of a bind.'

Eden closed her eyes momentarily. Knowing her friend like she did, the whole visit had been leading up to this. She knew something was about to be said that wasn't good. 'What's happened?'

'I've quarrelled with Carleton.' Annabella straightened, held her chin high. 'I'll not apologise for it. It's his doing. I won't live with his mother and I told him so.'

'And?'

'Well…'

Eden stared at her with a raised eyebrow.

Annabella jerked to her feet and strode to the window, kicking out her skirts as she did so. 'I told Carleton I wished to live here at Bradbury Hall and that he must come here too.'

'His response?'

'He refused.' Annabella looked out the window, which overlooked lawns and gardens. 'I won't live at his farm. It's beneath me to do so and horrid of him to insist.'

'It's hardly a simple farm cottage now, is it?' Eden stood and joined her at the window. 'The house is very large and well situated on the rise. They have servants—'

'It's his mother's house and he's at her beck and call each moment of the day.'

'You exaggerate surely. He is the master. It's his house.' Eden moved back to the table to pick up her teacup and take a sip.

'She pulls his strings as though he was a puppet. His mother telegrammed him every week and wrote enormous letters to him. In turn, he would stay up for hours writing to her about business matters he never mentioned to me.'

'They have been a team for so long, dearest. It would be hard for him to break away when he's been the only male in the family for the last ten years.'

Annabella stiffened. 'He broke a promise.'

'Darling, come sit down and finish your tea.' Eden sat once more and held out her hand for Annabella, as though she was a child. Had their roles always been thus? Eden couldn't recall ever feeling so much older than Annabella before. Yes, there were a few years difference in their ages, but now it seemed decades. The sisterhood she once felt had changed to something closer to mother and daughter.

'Oh, Eden.' Annabella sighed heavily and returned to her chair. 'Carleton said, no, *promised* me, he'd buy us a house in York. Now he won't. He says the farm is where we shall live. Why? I *don't* understand. He's not needed there. Between his overseer and his mother, it all runs smoothly.'

'Can't you perhaps try it for a while, just to see if you like it?'

'No. I won't bring up my baby there with his mother watching over me.'

Eden stared. 'Baby?'

Dropping her gaze, Annabella nodded. 'Yes. I think I'm three months with child.'

'Dearest, that is wonderful news.' Eden gripped her hands. 'Exactly what this family needs. Are you excited?'

'I'm frightened to death. Completely terrified. I didn't want this to happen, at least not yet, not for years.' Annabella's blue eyes filled with tears. 'I won't go to the farm. Promise you'll help me to stay here.'

'Your husband will want you beside him at such a time.'

Annabella raised her chin. 'He doesn't know, and I won't tell him while ever he's being so stubborn.'

'You must tell him. Besides you can't hide it forever.' Eden wryly shook her head. 'If you tell him, he might grant you your wish.'

'No, he's a brute and I hate him.'

Eden leaned back in her chair and studied her friend. 'Why are you acting like a spoilt child? You're a grown woman, married and with a child on the way. What has become of the Annabella I loved? You've turned into this whining ungrateful girl I barely know.'

A tear trickled over her pale cheek. 'It's all gone bad, horribly bad. I married the wrong man, Eden.'

114

She looked at Annabella as though she had spoken a foreign language. But for the first time since her return, Eden saw the true Annabella Bradbury escaping from the flippertigibbert that had arrived an hour ago. 'Anna—'

'No, hear me out.' Annabella rose and went back to the window. 'I thought I loved Carleton, truly I did. But while on our honeymoon I...' She hung her head.

Worried, Eden rose and went to her. 'What is it?'

'Carleton spent so much time away from me, chasing his own interests. It's amazing really. The man had never left England before our honeymoon, but the minute he's on the ship, he's talking to all these gentlemen and becomes absorbed in business issues.'

'Many men enjoy business.'

'He's a farmer. Yes, he's not without means, but at the base of it he's a moorland farmer with no knowledge of the business world.' Annabella twisted her handkerchief. 'He wants to pretend to be of a higher class than he is. An equal to Papa, Joel and Charlie. Only money doesn't make the man. My Papa said that many times when faced with some tradesman with a sovereign in his pocket.'

'I think you're being a little harsh. Carleton is not some uneducated cottage dweller. He has a fine house and land. He's educated and clever.'

'And now he wants to join the commercial ranks. He'll be laughed at. I know he will. It was embarrassing watching him hanging onto the coat tails of the gentlemen on board ship. He fawned over them, wanting their advice and help on how to make enormous amounts of money in different ventures.'

Eden frowned at her scathing tone. 'What is so wrong with him wanting to better himself and his family?'

'He doesn't need to better me! I'm a Bradbury. He did extremely well to catch me. I could have had anyone.'

The urge to slap her arrogant face was tempting, but Eden held back. 'As I recall there were hordes of young men wanting your hand. So, if you could have had anyone, why did you choose him?'

'I saw him as a dashing man, who adored me. No one is as handsome as Carleton.'

'Come now, I don't believe for a minute you are that shallow.'

Annabella turned away. 'Then perhaps you don't know me very well at all.'

'Nonsense. No one knows you better than me.' Eden stared at her back. 'You were totally in love with him. You begged your father to let you marry him, even though the Colonel wanted more for you, someone of a higher class.'

'Father's choices were old men, or ugly young ones. No amount of money and privilege would have induced me marry any of them.'

Eden folded her arms, tired of Annabella's selfishness. 'Then why are saying such things about the man you *did* accept?'

Strolling to the fireplace, Annabella stared down into the empty grate. 'He became different, a stranger to me. Everywhere we went he obsessed on the money side of things. I don't understand why, Papa had paid for everything. Carleton hardly had to resort to using his own money at all.'

'Perhaps that was the problem. He might have felt belittled.'

'Why should he? Many a man would be grateful.'

'None of the things you've mentioned so far give cause for such censure.'

Annabella banged her palm on the mantelpiece. 'You don't understand. He had no consideration for me. In every port, in every city, he left me alone so he could pursue his own interests. How could he do that? It was our *honeymoon*!' Sobs racked her body. She hunched over, crying as though her heart would break.

'Darling.' Eden drew her into her embrace. 'Shh now. You're home and perhaps Carleton will try to win your favour again, but to do so you must discuss this with him. He may not even be aware of your feelings in this regard.'

'No!' Annabella backed away, her eyes wide and frightened. 'I cannot speak of it.'

'Why? He must be made to understand.'

'It leads to quarrels. Terrible arguments.' Annabella glanced away, a blush creeping up her neck.

The sense of unease remained with Eden as she watched Annabella dab at her eyes and nose. There was more to this, she could feel it. 'What did you do while Carleton followed his business contacts?'

Annabella raised her chin, all sign of tears gone. 'Amused myself.' Her icy tone cut across the room.

'Alone?' Eden wondered whether Annabella had curbed her ability for flirtations.

'Sometimes. However, I made friends easily. I always have done, you know that. I'm happy to make up a number in any party.'

The door opened and Charlie walked in, smiling. 'There you both are.' He glanced at Eden and then kissed Annabella's cheek. 'I'm so happy you're home. I've had a nap and now full of energy to hear all your news.'

'Oh, splendid.' Annabella took his hand led him over to the chairs. 'I'll order more tea for us.'

Eden stepped forward. 'I'll arrange for fresh tea, but I can't stay. I've my duties to see to before I leave to go home.'

Annabella pouted. 'Home? You aren't staying?'

'I don't live in. The girls need me at home.'

'But I need you, too.'

Shaking her head, Eden sighed. 'You are a grown woman, Annabella, my girls are not.' She walked out of the room and along the hall towards the kitchen.

'Eden,' Charlie called.

She turned and walked back to him. 'Yes? Is there something you need me to do before I go?'

'No.' He frowned and glanced back at the room they'd just left. 'What happened between you two? I could detect a tension when I came in.'

'That's because Annabella has changed, or maybe I have. I don't know.' She shrugged. 'Suddenly I see her selfishness more prominently than ever before. I love her like a sister, but there are times I don't like her. I didn't really acknowledge that until this afternoon.'

'That's a bit cruel. We all know Annabella can be spirited, but she isn't unkind.' Eden kissed his cheek.

'You're too loyal for your own good sometimes. I'll not dissect Annabella's character with you. It's a waste of time.'

'This is unlike you, my dear.'

Sighing, Eden fingered the bunch of keys at her waist. 'I'm tired, Charlie, forgive me.'

His face softened. 'You're doing too much. All this cleaning and running two homes. I should never have asked you to take this role. I suppose I too am selfish.'

Emotion tightened her throat at his caring. 'It is nothing, really. I'm missing Nathan, that's all. I always had him to talk to. I miss being held.'

'Yes, of course.' He took her hand and kissed it. 'You can always talk to me.'

'Indeed.' She kissed his cheek. 'Ignore my bad temper. Annabella's return has reminded me of other times, before she married, when I was happier.'

They turned as Annabella stood in the doorway. 'Forgive me, Eden. You know I would never wish to upset you. I love you as a sister.'

Eden nodded, her throat tight with tears.

Charlie patted her hand. 'Shall we have a picnic tomorrow? Bring the girls Eden. Let us forget our roles in life for one day and eat and lie in the sun. Yes?'

'Very well.' Leaving them, Eden headed for the housekeeper's room and tried not to think of the last picnic she went on, when Nathan had been with her.

Chapter 11

Heaving rain blighted the landscape beyond the drawing room window. Eden sighed and moved away towards the fireplace, where a blaze roared.

'Are the girls very disappointed about the picnic cancellation?' Charlie glanced up from his newspaper.

'Yes, but Grandfather promised to help them make gingerbread. That appeased them.'

'I really wanted to spend the day with them.'

'They were excited too, but there will be other opportunities once the weather warms.'

'I wrote to Joel last evening and mentioned spending the day with the girls. How odd it is that he's not seen them. He would love them I think.'

'He's been gone so long I imagine we are all strangers to him now.' She looked away, her heart hurting. Once she had dreamed her children would be Joel's too. It seemed a lifetime ago. What did he think of her now? Would he forgive her marriage to Nathan? Would he care?

'The news is the war won't continue for much longer. It's time he came home. I won't last forever.'

She rested her hand on the back of his chair. 'Do you need anything?'

'No, nothing at all. Except perhaps a smile from you.'

She smiled automatically and squeezed his shoulder. 'What time will Annabella be home?'

'Soon. She didn't want to go out in this weather, but Carleton insisted.' Charlie folded the newspaper and placed it on the occasional table beside the chair. 'I never expected Carleton to be the domineering type. He never looks at Annabella unless it's with a scowl. Does love diminish so soon after a honeymoon?'

Stepping to the hearth, she took the poker and shifted the logs. Sparks shot up the chimney. 'I believe not all went well on the honeymoon. Annabella hinted things didn't go as planned and that Carleton changed.'

'She married him too quickly. Both father and I said the same to her. They could have afforded to wait a year to become more used to one another.'

'True, but you know how impulsive she is.'

'He wouldn't have treated her cruelly, would he?'

'Only in a silent, disapproving way I should imagine.'

'What can we do about it? Obviously, she refuses to live at his home, which is likely to cause unpleasantness. Can we help in any way? Father or Joel would have known what to do.'

'She must learn by her own mistakes, Charlie. She is no longer a child.'

'Yes, I know, but she is the youngest and we've all protected her. I should have realised last night that she wasn't herself. She hardly ate. However, I was so tired I had to retire after dinner.' Charlie stood and leaned an elbow on the mantelpiece. 'She may have wanted to talk, to confide, and yet I went to bed early like an old man.'

'Don't blame yourself. Time alone might be just what she needs.'

He sighed and nodded. 'I'll be in the study if you need me. Those accounts are never ending.'

'I'll bring you in a cup of tea shortly.'

At the door, he paused and rubbed his chin. 'Perhaps we should have a small dinner party to celebrate her return, what do you think? Nothing grand, just something simple and intimate.'

'I'll ask her. See if she's up to it.'

'Good. We all need cheering up.' He smiled and left the room.

After placing the fireguard on the hearth, Eden glanced around to make sure all was neat in case someone should call. Leaving the drawing room, she then went down the hall and turned into the service corridor. She spent ten minutes in the kitchen conversing with Cook, making sure all was in order and then entered the housekeeper's rooms, which consisted of a small sitting room and bedroom off from the corridor. Although Eden didn't use the bedroom, the sitting had become her one place to take a few minutes rest or to write accounts and wages. In here she also talked with the staff. Most afternoons Mellors joined her for a cup of tea, while Charlie napped.

Before sitting at her desk, she checked the vase of daffodils sitting on the square table by the window had enough water. She inhaled their scent and smiled at how they brightened the room.

When the door opened, she turned expecting Mellors, but her stomach plummeted to her shoes as Clifton filled the doorway. 'Get out.'

'Now is that anyway to treat me?'

'No, it's better than you deserve. You should be horse whipped.'

He laughed and advanced into the room. 'Haven't you missed me at all?'

She swallowed back her fear. 'Not in the least. Why should I?'

'I've been gone some months. Did you wonder when I'd return?'

'I've been praying you'll be trampled on by a horse and carriage or fall in front of a train. Will that do?'

'Your spirit always gladdens my heart. It's so refreshing in a woman.' He paused and gazed around the room. 'Fleming has been in touch with me. Filled me in on what's been happening here.' Clifton touched some of the papers on her desk. 'I decided it was time to visit again. Charlie's temper is bound to have diminished by now. He too kindhearted to hold a grudge for long.'

She watched him prowl around the room, wishing to god that he'd suffer a fatal heart seizure and rid her of his presence. He'd put on more weight, his face puffy and eyes bloodshot.

Clifton walked closer and she shrank from him as he lightly touched her cheek. 'You are very beautiful, Eden. A true woman of passion.' His small eyes narrowed with yearning. 'Despite your treatment of me, I have always loved you, wanted you.'

'You know nothing of love or kindness.'

'Because you never gave me the chance. However, I forgive you. You saw only Joel. Yet what did he do? Leave you. I won't do that.' His face lowered to kiss her.

She twisted away, disgust filling her. 'Don't touch me.'

His fingers curled around her chin, forcing her to look at him. 'I am aware that you were behind Charlie's offensive letter.'

'What-what Charlie does is entirely up to him.' She tore out of his grip and glared. 'If your behaviour induces him to write scolding letters to you as though he was your parent, then that's hardly my fault.'

'Although I admire your strength of character you won't make him reject me, he's too loyal to his family.'

'Loyalty doesn't make him blind to all things, Clifton. You can only push so far.'

'Perhaps I should test that theory…' An evil smile lit his face. He leaned closer, pressing her backwards. His lips fleetingly touched hers and she shuddered. 'Until now I've done exactly as I pleased and received no more than worded censure in a letter.'

'Doesn't your conscience ever trouble you?' She tried not to gag. Panic and revulsion churned her stomach.

'Never.' Chuckling, he took a step back and straightened his waistcoat. 'Speaking of conscience, don't think in my absence that I forgot about Josephine. Your husband's death will not alter the fact that she is mine and I want her with me. As her father I will do my duty to her and you.'

'Prove she's yours. It's your word against mine.'

He blanched at her dare. 'Will you and your grandfather swear under oath in a court of law that Josephine is Nathan's?'

'Without a moment's hesitation.'

'Are you willing for this to turn ugly. For the whole district to know you laid with me? I will tell everyone we had an affair and that you enjoyed being my whore. How will people look upon you when they learn you have lain with me and then hoodwinked the saintly Nathan Harris? Mud sticks once spread, Eden, you know that.'

'And what will that serve?' She mocked him. 'Do you believe I will simply hand my daughter over to you? Are you insane? I care nothing for others' opinions.'

'What of this family?' He swung his podgy arms wide, encompassing the room and all it entailed. 'Will you let the Bradbury name be dragged down with your reputation? What will Charlie, Annabella and Joel think of you then?'

She stepped forward, brave in her anger, an anger, which threatened to choke her. 'Even if you were to *kill* me, you'd still not have her. The Bradburys are my daughters' sponsors. Anything happens to me and the girls go to them. Will you kill all your cousins too?'

'I am no simpleton.' He hesitated, looked down at his shoes and then back to her. 'That is why we are going to be married.'

Her eyes widened. 'Married. Me and you?' The desire to laugh in his face was barely contained.

Sighing, he nodded and strolled back to the door, his hands clasped behind his back. 'Yes. We will marry, that way I will have my daughter and hopefully you'll produce a son too.'

He was mad. Yet, his madness frightened her senseless. Too many times she's seen the results of his lunacy. Pretending to be unaffected, she scoffed at his ridiculousness and cocked her head to one side. 'No. We won't be married.'

'If you do not marry me, then I'll make sure you never see Josephine again.' The menacing words were quietly spoken and lingered in the air. 'I don't make idle threats, my dear, you should know that by now.' His gaze, filled with desire, roamed over her.

Eden reached behind her and gripped the table for support. Clifton sauntered out of the room and at the same time Annabella's voice drifted down the corridor.

'Clifton. Why I didn't know you were here. Delightful to see you, Cousin. Another face is always needed at the dining table. I was looking for Eden, but now you're here I can show you the present I bought you. I also bought a beautiful fan for Aunt Ada. You will give it to her for me, won't you? How is she?' The chatter ebbed away as they returned up the corridor. Silence descended in the housekeeper's room and Eden sagged in relief.

She knew with experience that Clifton would carry out his threat. A moan escaped and she covered her mouth with her hand. She had to tell Charlie. No. She shook the thought away instantly. He was too weak to deal with such news and would he believe her? She hardly believed it herself. Clifton and her? Married? Charlie would think Clifton was being kind in offering marriage to her — a widow with two fatherless girls.

Hysterical laughter bubbled up inside her chest, but it soon turned to dry sobs. If she'd told Charlie at the beginning when Clifton first attacked her, then none of this would be happening now. He'd have been an outcast. Disowned by the family. But she had kept silent and let them think she'd loved Nathan for some time and marrying him was normal. She lied convincingly enough for them to forget that the only man she'd loved was Joel.

If only the Colonel had rejected Clifton from the family that fatal day…

If only Nathan had lived…

Her mind whirled, but amidst it all, she knew what she had to do.

Pushing away from the table she crossed to the desk and unlocked the top drawer. At the back was a large pouch of money to pay any stray tradesman's account or something unexpected. Six pounds. She had counted it yesterday. Tucking it into her skirt pocket, she glanced around for any of her personal items. Nothing. All her correspondence was to do with housekeeping. Satisfied she'd left nothing behind, she hurried to the door, grabbed her black shawl from the hook behind and wrapped it around her shoulders.

She dashed into the kitchen and passed her housekeeping keys over to Cook, the only staff member trusted with them. Cutting short enquires and declining to have a cup of tea, Eden told Cook she had to go home because of a headache. Once out the back door, she forced herself to walk calmly passed the service buildings, the stables and through the sodden gardens.

At the gate to the deer park, she stopped and turned, her heart beating in her ears. Beyond the dripping trees, Bradbury Hall shimmered in the afternoon sun that broke through the rain clouds. Tears quivered on her lashes as she recorded the house, and more importantly the beloved people within, to memory.

She would never see them again.

Wrenching away, she cried all the way across the field to the wood. Once in the dark interior, she blindly followed the winding path to the cottage. She had to shut her mind to what she was leaving behind, but it was too much to take in. Falling against a tree trunk, she sobbed and wailed out her pain and cursed the fates that had dealt her such a heavy hand.

Sometime later, she straightened and wiped her eyes on a handkerchief pulled from her pocket. The pouch of money banged gently against her thigh, reminding her of the job ahead. With a final sniff, she tucked her handkerchief away and lifted her head proudly. She may have lost Joel, Nathan and now her way of life, but she'd not lose her daughters. Rage replaced the heart-twisting misery and she strode towards the cottage.

At the front door, she paused slightly, but continued in and smiled brightly at her daughters, who sat in front of the fire drawing with charcoal and paper.

'Ma! Ma!' They jumped up to hug her and she kissed their heads.

'I have a surprise for you both. Your Uncle Charlie has given me permission to take a small holiday and you're coming with me.'

The girls squealed and clapped and over their heads Eden gazed at her grandfather's shocked face. She pushed the girls over to the ladder. 'Go up and gather your things. One bag of clothes only, and pack a toy or two, or a book. Nothing too heavy mind.'

Once they had clambered excitedly up the ladder and out of view, Eden collapsed at Grandfather's feet and buried her head on his lap. She didn't cry, all her tears were gone. Instead she closed her eyes and held her darling grandfather tight.

'He's come back I take it,' Grandfather said after some moments.

She nodded; her throat closed.

'And you didn't tell Master Charlie?'

'No. How could I? He's sick, Grandfather, and lucky if he lasts the next winter. How can I burden him more?'

Grandfather stroked her hair. 'I always knew this day would come when he drove you from your home.'

She raised her face. 'I have to go. There's no other way. Clifton's threatened that if I don't marry him, I'll never see Josephine again. And he'll do it, we know the evil he's capable of. In a blink of an eye he'd steal her and be gone forever. I can't take that chance.'

'No of course you can't.' Grandfather slowly creaked to his feet and hobbled over to the dresser along the wall.

Eden stood. 'I know at your age moving to another place will be difficult, but—'

'I'm not going with you.'

She stared at him. 'What do you mean? I can't leave without you.'

'Yes, you must.' He opened a drawer and shuffled items about. 'I will only slow you down.'

'You can't slow me down. We'll be travelling by train. You can sit on a train just as you can sit in this cottage.'

Grandfather took out a tin and handed it to her. 'I'm too old to be running from vermin like Clifton. I'll stay here. This is my home and he's not driving me from it. But you must go. I can't protect you here.'

She thrust the tin back to him. 'I'll not take our money. You have no way of earning more. I can get a job once I'm settled.'

'Eden,' his voice broke as he gripped her hands in his arthritic ones. 'Listen to me, my love. Out there, is a garden full of vegetables growing, plus hens, ducks, eggs and I can still manage to trap a rabbit. In the cupboard are jars of pickles, jam and much more. I'll manage, lass.' He put the tin on the table. 'You will need it more than me.'

The girls scampered down the ladder, laughing and talking. Their noise jerked Eden into action. She hurried up into the loft and quickly packed her own bag. Downstairs once more, she found Grandfather had filled a small hamper basket with food and drink for the journey.

He ushered the girls in front of him while he carried the hamper. On the doorstep, he passed it to Eden, who carried it and her own bag. 'Now, lass. Make sure you write, but don't send it here. Send it to Earnshaw. I'll let him know what's going on.'

She nodded, dreading having to say goodbye. 'Once we have a place, I'll let you know, and you can come to us for a while.'

'Aye, I'll do that. Have you somewhere in mind?'

'No. I'll see where the train takes us.'

'Good idea. Try the cities, you can get lost easily in a city.'

'And there'll be more work there too.'

'I'll go across to the Hall tomorrow and tell them you won't be coming back. That will give you a head start from Clifton should he come after you.'

'Yes.' Eden bowed her head. 'I hope Charlie and Annabella will forgive me. I'm not a coward am I, Grandfather, for running away?'

'Nay, don't be so daft, lass. You're protecting the girls from a madman. You've the courage of a lion and I'll not have you think the opposite.' He looked up at the misty rain falling. 'Wrap up well. This rain will last into the night.'

'It won't take us long to walk to the station.' She kissed his stubble-covered cheek. 'So this isn't goodbye, just farewell for a few weeks.'

'Aye, lass.' He smiled and bent to kiss the girls. 'Take care of your mother and behave yourselves.'

The girls smothered him with kisses and made him promise to look after the animals for them.

Eden held him tight. 'I love you.'

'And you too, my lass. Now go before it's dark. You don't want to miss the last train.'

With the girls skipping ahead, Eden glanced back and smiled in farewell to her beloved grandfather and her home. For a moment her legs wouldn't move. She couldn't leave her home, the wood, the Hall. All this was her world, all she'd ever known.

'Come on, Ma!' Josephine called; her face bright with excitement.

Eden looked at her and thought of Clifton touching her, announcing that this beautiful girl was a product of him. She shivered. He would have to kill her first.

After a final wave, she settled the hamper and her bag more comfortably in her hands and head held high, she followed the girls down the path. At the side of the cottage, they took the fork to the right that led to Gargrave and the train station, which would take them to a new life.

Chapter 12

Grandfather waited by the side of the stables and watched the yard. The grey cloud from yesterday lingered, but so far this morning no rain had fallen. One of the Bradbury's grooms, busy at work cleaning out the stables, whistled at a scurrying maid, who carried baskets of clothes to the laundry.

'Horatio, what the 'ell you doing?'

Grandfather spun around, his hand on his heart. 'Jesus, Barney, you nearly did me in then. You can't sneak up on an old man like that.'

'I'm sorry, friend, but I thought I was seeing things.' Barney pushed his flat cap back on his head. 'What you doing here?'

'Watching for Clifton.' He leaned heavily on his walking stick. 'I need to speak with Master Charlie, but not while *he's* there.'

Nodding, Barney scratching his chin. 'Wait here. I'll see if any orders have come down yet.' He disappeared around the corner of the stable block. He'd only been gone a minute or two before he was back. 'Clifton's ordered the carriage to be brought round the front of the house for nine o'clock. Want to wait it out or come back after he's gone?'

'I'll stay. It took me long enough to walk to here. I can't make the trip twice.'

'Come, let's us have a cuppa in the kitchen. Cook will give us some breakfast.'

Hobbling across the yard, Horatio gazed around and remembered his time working here. Nothing much physically had changed, but the atmosphere had. Gone was the jovial environment and the hubbub of activity. Back then the Hall had double the number of servants to care for a large family. Now, everything had diminished, the servants and family. A pall of gloom seemed to hover over the house, and it had nothing to do with the miserable weather.

Inside the kitchen, Cook, with her kind rounded face, welcomed the men in and hustled them to sit down. Moments later, she was placing bowls of porridge and large plates of bacon, kidneys and bread before them. Despite the serious nature of his business, Horatio ate well, knowing he'd not have a meal that size again for some time.

The door leading to the corridor opened and Mellors stepped down into the kitchen. He frowned seeing Horatio. 'This is a surprise, Mr Morley. Is everything well at home?'

'Eden won't be in today.' Horatio swallowed the last of his bread and took a sip of tea to help it go down. 'I'm to see Master Charlie. Is he available this morning?'

'Why...er, yes. I am sure he is.' Mellors rubbed his chin. 'Give me a minute to find out.' He looked at Barney and Cook waiting, their expressions keen. 'Would you care to come and wait in the study?'

'Aye, mighty kind of you.' Horatio followed Mellors into the corridor and through to the study where he was left alone. He'd been in this room once before, when the Colonel had been a youth and his father owned the Hall. Again, nothing much had changed in the room, the same half-timbered walls with red wall-paper above, heavy framed country scenes, and thick solid furniture. A man's room.

The door opened and Horatio braced himself to part his news, but as Annabella rushed in all smiles and bouncing lace, his carefully prepared speech left his head.

'Why, Mr Morley, Mellors just told me you were here. How lovely to see you?' She kissed his whisk-ered cheek. 'I was telling Eden that I must call in and share a cup of your lovely ginger ale.'

He smiled. This delightful girl never changed. She was like another granddaughter to him, for she'd spent a lot of her time growing up at the cottage with Eden. Inseparable they were. 'How are you Miss An-nabella? Sorry, Mrs Carleton.'

'I insist you called me Miss Annabella forever. Mrs Carleton makes me sound like an old madam and I refuse to grow older.' She laughed. 'Now what is this about Eden? Is she sick?' Annabella turned to sit on a chair placed between two large bookcases. 'She works far too hard, you know.'

'Aye—'

The door opened again, and Charlie walked in, his hand held out to Horatio. 'Mr Morley. A delight to see you, sir.'

'And you, Master Charlie.' Horatio was shocked to see the change in the young man. He looked to be for-ty-eight instead of twenty-eight. His skin had a yel-low-grey tinge, his eyes sunken.

'Please, take a seat.' He waved Horatio into a chair near the desk. Despite his illness, Charlie walked up-right with purpose strides, as though defying the sick-ness to cower him. He sat behind the desk on the large leather winged chair. 'What is this about Eden? Is she ill?'

'No, not ill.' He cleared his throat and looked from Charlie to Annabella and back again. When he had left the cottage this morning, he had every intention to lie to them, to tell them Eden had taken the girls to the seaside for a few days. The excuse was flimsy enough, he knew, but he'd been prepared to lie through his teeth. Only now, faced with their trusting faces, he found he couldn't lie to them.

'What is it?' Charlie's face paled. 'Something has happened, hasn't it?'

'Yes.'

Annabella jerked in her chair. 'Oh, no.'

Charlie folded his arms on the desk. 'May we have all the details, Horatio?'

'I don't think you will like them, Master Charlie.'

'Nevertheless.'

'Eden has taken the girls and left. She's left for good.'

'But why?' Annabella gasped. 'She never mentioned any of this to me. I don't understand. Eden would never do such a thing. Why would she go?'

'Because she's been threatened.'

'By whom?' Charlie's voice was low and intimidating, at that moment he looked like his brother, Joel, and sounded like the Colonel.

He glanced at Annabella. 'I will tell you both of what's occurred because I feel you need to know, though Eden may never forgive me for doing so.' He paused and took a breath, then he began from the beginning — the day their cousin raped his beautiful Eden in the wood.

~ ~ ~

Eden grasped Lillie's hand and gripped her bag tighter as they stepped from the train. Despite the muted lights of the cavernous station the night's shadows made the platform eerie. The lateness of the train meant there were small crowds and Eden ushered the tired girls out of the station with ease. Once out on the street, the old castle walls loomed before them and she stopped under a gaslight to gather her bearings.

York. She'd been once before, many years ago with Annabella and the Colonel. They'd spent three days touring around York, going to the theatre, shopping and dining. It'd been a seventeenth birthday present for Annabella from her father. How long ago it seemed now.

'Where will we go, Ma?' Josephine sighed. As darkness had descended outside the train windows, the girls' excitement had waned also.

Not that she could blame them. They'd travelled by train to Leeds and then waited an hour before they could catch the next train going to York. 'We'll find a place to stay for the night. There's bound to be some lodgings close by.'

'I'm hungry.' Lillie grumbled and yawned.

'Yes, pet. I know.' Determined not to be cowed under by the enormity of what she'd done, Eden marched the girls across the street and around the corner.

A hansom cab driver was dropping off a client and Eden hurried up to him. 'Excuse me. Do you know of some lodging nearby for me and my daughters?'

The old driver scratched his head under his cap. 'Behind you is Tam Corbett's lodgings for men.'

Eden turned and looked at the two-story tenement house.

'You can't go in there, but there's Mrs Prim down the end of this street on the right. Last house. Can't miss it. Or there's more further away. Several, in fact. All within a mile of walking in any direction. Jane Ackroyd runs a good house in Nunnery lane. I'd try there first, or even Booths in Monkgate.'

'Mrs Prim's lodging will do for tonight, if it's clean. If not, I'll try the others in Nunnery lane and...'

'Monkgate.'

'Monkgate. Thank you.'

'Bea Prim is clean and a stickler for rules. I've heard no complaints yet and I've been working this side of York for twenty years.'

'Thank you for your help.'

He doffed his cap and gathered the horse's reins. 'Good night to you then.' With a click of his teeth, he drove the horse on.

Smiling at the girls, Eden ushered them down the street. A drunken man leant heavily against a lamp post on the other side of the road, singing loudly. Suddenly, he opened his trousers and urinated into the gutter. Eden was unsuccessful in shielding the girls from the spectacle. Halfway down the street, an alley cut off to the right. As they passed it, a cat yowled and there came a clatter of running feet. Lillie squeaked and huddled against Eden. She hugged them closer and quickened their pace. She didn't care what the fee was at the lodgings; she wasn't staying out on the street any longer than necessary.

Pausing at the last house on the right, she guided them up the stone steps to the front door. A brass plate nailed to the wall beside the door announced, 'Prim's Lodging House'. Eden rapped the door knocker and waited. After a minute and no one had answered, she thought perhaps it was too late and Mrs Prim had closed her door for the night.

'Ma, I need the pot.' Josephine screwed up her face and jiggled on the spot.

'Hold on.' Eden rapped again, praying someone would answer. She didn't want to trudge the streets to find another lodging.

At last noise came from the other side and the door inched open. A young man stuck his head out and blinked. 'Mother sick.'

Frowning, Eden stepped forward. 'Is there a room to rent? Just for tonight?'

The door opened wider and the youth thrust out his hand. 'Pleased to meet you.'

Eden shook his hand. 'There is a room?'

'Laurence Prim.' He smiled, straightening to his full height of at least six feet.

The vacant gaze in his pale blue eyes gave Eden the clue that he might be a simpleton. 'Is Mrs Prim in?'

He opened the door wider and let them in. 'Mother sick.' He put his finger to his lips. 'Shhh.'

'Who do I see about a room then?' Eden looked around the narrow hall and the staircase going up to the next floor. A cold draught swept around their ankles and she shivered. No lamp was lit to banish the gloom, but light spilled from an open doorway further down the hallway.

'Mother sick.'

With a sigh, Eden rubbed her forehead. 'Is there anyone else here?'

Laurence scowled and twisted his fingers together as though in torment. 'Mother sick. I make tea.' He grinned.

Josephine giggled and Eden glared at her.

'Laurie?' A croaky voice called from the top of the stairs. A grey-haired woman stood bent over the rail. Wrapped in a long thick shawl, she held a candle.

Eden stepped forward and gazed up. 'Good evening. I'm sorry to disturb you. Are you Mrs Prim? I'm in need of a room for the night for me and my two daughters.'

'I'm closed to guests, I'm afraid.' The candlelight wavered as Mrs Prim coughed.

'We won't be any trouble. I promise.' Eden placed a hand on the banister. 'It's getting too late to walk the streets with the girls. We may be turned away from other places at this time of the night.'

'None of the beds are aired. I'm not prepared…' Prim coughed again, struggling for breath. 'You must go. I can't help you.'

Instinct made Eden climb the stairs. 'I don't mind making our bed. My girls are so tired they'd sleep on the floor if need be.' The closer she came to Bea Prim, the sorrier she felt for the woman, who was grey with exhaustion. 'Please let us stay. In return I can help look after you.'

'Laurence can look after me,' she snapped. 'We do all right as we are.'

'When did you last eat a proper meal?'

Mrs Prim glared at her, then another coughing fit shook she slight frame. Eden hurried up the last remaining steps and grabbed the candle off the woman before she dropped it. 'Go back to bed. You'll not get well standing on a cold landing. Is there a fire lit in your room?'

'No. Haven't been well enough to pay the coalman.'

'How long have you been ill?'

'I've been really bad, nigh on two weeks. Can't seem to shift it from my chest.'

'Have you been two weeks without guests?'

'Aye.'

Eden smiled in sympathy and patted the woman's arm. 'I'm Eden Harris. My girls and I are looking for a place to stay for a while. I'd be happy to help run the place, until you get back on your feet.'

Bea Prim, with her small dark eyes, gazed at her suspiciously. 'What do you know about keeping a house? I run a tidy business, no riff-raff.'

'I've been a housekeeper before, Mrs Prim. I assure you I am clean and honest.' Eden prayed she wouldn't want references or the name of her last employment. She had thought about changing her name but knew the girls wouldn't be able to understand or keep their real name a secret for long.

'I can't pay you a wage. We're not earning owt as it is.'

'Lodgings and board will be payment enough to start with.'

'I'm Bea Prim and we'll give it a trial to the end of the week. I should be better by then.'

'Fair enough.'

Pointing a thin finger at a door on the right of the landing, Bea sniffed. 'That room has a double bed in it. Will you all fit?'

'We'll make do.'

Bea nodded to a large built-in cupboard on their left. 'All the sheets and pillowcases are in there. Downstairs, at the end of the hall, is the kitchen. Make yourself some tea. I've not been downstairs for two weeks, I've no idea what food Laurence has bought.' At that, Bea seemed to wilt, tiredness overwhelming her.

'Come, Mrs Prim, let's get you back into bed and then I'll make you a cup of tea.' Eden led her back to the only bedroom with the door open.

'Hah, I doubt we have any.'

The following morning, Eden rose early and dressed quietly, not wanting to wake the girls up. Dawn had broken and beyond the window came the street noises of people going to work. After washing her face in the cold water, she brought up last night, she tiptoed out of the room. On the landing, she listened for any sound from the other rooms. Silence. Bea had coughed all night, but hopefully slept well now.

Downstairs, Eden entered the kitchen and shivered in the chill. By candlelight the previous evening, she had managed to make cups of tea for everyone, with the remaining tealeaves found in a tin. Now though, as the rising sun shone through the dirty window, the state of the kitchen became clear. Used plates, cups, food scraps and empty bottles littered the large table in the middle of the room. Newspapers and correspondence lay on the stone flagged floor. Muddy footprints left a trail from the scullery door over to the chair by the range. The range itself needed a good black leading, and upon opening the oven door, Eden winced at the amount of ashes piled up.

She turned and went through to the scullery. Clothes and sheets filled the huge copper pot. Stacked in the corner was a large dustbin of stinking rubbish.

Eden returned to the kitchen and went through the hallway and entered the first of the two rooms on this floor. The front room seemed to be a communal sitting room. A bow window overlooked the street. An upright piano was against one wall next to a large bookcase filled with books and newspaper periodicals. Two red velvet sofas and a few easy chairs were placed about the room to give guests a place to sit and read or to converse as the mood took them.

The second room was smaller, and obviously the dining room. It held a long narrow table seating twelve chairs. The vase of flowers in the middle of it needed replacing, for the dead petals had dropped over the polished timber. A servery stood against the wall that joined the two rooms.

'Breakfast?'

Eden jumped and spun around. Laurence stood in the doorway smiling. 'Oh, you gave me a fright.'

'I go to market and buy eggs?' He blinked, his expression like that of an expectant five-year-old.

'Well, yes...' She went back into the kitchen and into the pantry beside the scullery. Not all the shelves were bare, some contained jars of pickles, small sacks of flour, coffee and sugar and there was a hunk of bread and a triangle of cheese. Nothing much to tempt the appetite.

'We have bacon too?' Laurence grinned, standing right behind her.

'Do you have money?'

He frowned and scratched the side of his nose. 'Mother has.' He dashed out of the pantry up the hallway.

'No, wait!' She hurried after him. He stopped and looked at her strangely. From her pocket she took out a small leather bag that contained her money. 'I don't want your mother disturbed. She can pay me back later.'

'Eggs?' He held out his hand for the money.

'Yes, eggs, bacon and fresh bread. Oh, and tea leaves.' She went back to the kitchen with Laurence following her like a faithful dog. She unhooked a net bag from behind the back door. 'Take this. Now, can you remember it all?'

'Eggs.' He said proudly.

'Not just eggs. Bacon, bread and tea. I'll do more shopping this afternoon.'

He nodded and fetched his muddy boots from the scullery. After donning his boots and cap, he surprised her by kissing her cheek before rushing out of the back door. Through the window she watched him race out the back gate and into the cut running behind the buildings.

She shook her head, amazed at the situation she was in. Within twenty-four hours she had left the only home she'd known and walked straight into a lodging house needing her help. She'd planned to stay only one night and then move on, putting more distance between her and Clifton. Yet, how could she leave Mrs Prim, who was ill and alone with only her simple son to look after her? Perhaps she could stay for a week and see how the land lay after that. If she stayed inside and spoke to no one then Clifton wouldn't find her here. She was sure of that. A lodging house in the back streets of York just might be the ideal place to hide for a while until she decided what to do long term.

Taking a deep breath, Eden rolled up her sleeves. If she was going to help out for a few days, she might as well get started.

Chapter 13

I don't understand it.' Annabella kicked out her skirts at every turn as she paced the drawing room. 'This is madness. How could she do this to us? To frighten us so?'

'Calm down. Upsetting yourself won't make the situation better.' Charlie stood by the fireplace, one arm resting on the mantel.

'Nothing is making this situation better, is it? We've searched for three weeks for Eden and the girls and nothing. It's like they have disappeared into dust.' She balled her hands into fists. 'I could kill Clifton. I really could.'

Charlie nodded. 'He'll get what's coming to him, never fear. I have publicly denounced him as a cousin and made it known within certain business circles that he is no longer connected with the name Bradbury. I know it will hurt Aunt Ada, but it cannot be helped.'

She swore under her breath an unladylike word she'd heard the groomsmen say plenty of times. 'He's a cowardly monster. When I think of what he's done and how he shrugged it off when you confronted him. Well, it makes me sick.'

'Yes, a cad of the highest order. A brutal man. I'm ashamed to be related to such a person.'

'I never want to see him again, I'm telling you, as I won't be responsible for my actions.'

Charlie gave her a look of understanding. 'We won't see him again, I can assure you of that. He will never grace this house again with his presence and if I have my way, he'll be shunned by all of our friends and acquaintances.'

'Good.' Weary, Annabella sat on the sofa and sighed. 'I still can't believe it, you know. That such a thing happened, and we never knew, all this time. Poor Eden to suffer that and still have to face him whenever he stayed here. How did she cope with it?'

'I don't know.' Charlie shook his head, his hazel eyes sad. 'She's strong and admirable.'

'She should have told us.'

'I always looked upon her girls as my nieces, especially Josephine as I thought she was Joel's…'

'Joel's?'

'He loved her.'

Annabella stared at him. 'Really? I know Eden adored him and sometimes I sensed a feeling between them, but I never suspected more.'

'Joel hinted to me that it was impossible to become too attached to her, as father had made it clear she wasn't the bride he'd want for Joel. Father was worried family and friends would scorn Joel for marrying your companion. That's why Joel has stayed away. He couldn't have her, and to stay here and be in contact with her was too much for him.'

'But we all knew the army was for him.'

Charlie picked up a small, framed portrait of Joel that he had sat before he left for Africa. 'Yes, for a few years or so, but not for this long. Joel had other plans. He wanted to travel, to invest in schemes, improve the breed stock of the estate and so forth.'

'So, he stayed away because of Eden, because he couldn't have her.'

'Yes.' He sighed and placed the portrait back.

'Well, he needs to come home now.' Annabella rubbed her forehead, she felt so tired today. 'Does he still love her after all this time?'

'I don't know. Her marriage to Nathan shocked him.'

'Poor Joel and poor Eden. It's all so tragic and such a mess.'

'I don't blame Eden for keeping what happened a secret, but I do wish she had confided in me or you. One of us knowing would have helped her at times to get through it.'

'She had Nathan and her grandfather.' Annabella murmured. 'It is *now* that she needs us. Her grandfather is an old man and Nathan is gone. I can't bear to think of her out there alone with the girls.'

'I have people looking for her. It's all I can do until she contacts Horatio. He's promised to tell me where she is.'

Tears of shame welled in Annabella's eyes. 'I am a bad person, Charlie.'

'Why?'

'So many times, I've burdened Eden with my troubles and never once did I let her burden me. Never have I sat with her and asked her if she needed my help in anything. I never even thought to do so because she's always been so capable, so in control of everything. But that is no excuse. I should have asked. What kind of friend does that make me?'

'Bella—'

'Even my first day home, I was selfish, telling her my woes. What are they compared to the suffering she's had? Why didn't she ever tell me her secrets, her worries? Am I so stupid I cannot be trusted?'

'She loves you like a sister and no doubt wanted to protect you. How could she have come to us when it was *our* cousin who assaulted her? She knew the bind it would put us in. We'd have to take sides; it would have split the family.'

'I know that makes sense, but my heart hurts. I abused her love, the friendship she has always given me. I took it for granted.' Guilt twisted her stomach into knots. 'Have I always been such a terrible person, Charlie?'

He smiled and sat beside her on the sofa. 'No, dearest. You aren't a terrible person. A little self-involved at times, but not terrible.'

'I have made mistakes, Charlie, ones I'm not proud of.'

He took her hand. 'Everyone has. No one is perfect.'

She bowed her head and let the tears fall. 'On my honeymoon I laid with another man in revenge of Carleton's neglect of me. Now, I carry a child and I don't know who is the father.'

His hands tightened on hers. 'Oh, Bella.'

The sadness in his voice bowed her shoulders further. At that moment she wanted to crawl away and die somewhere quiet and dark. 'You cannot think worse of me than I do myself. I am not proud of my actions, but I had drunk too much wine and was upset. I wanted Carleton to notice that other men found me attractive, even if he no longer did. Only, it went too far and I ruined everything.'

'He shouldn't have neglected you.'

'I was trying to make him jealous, so he would forget his newfound interests and spend his time with me. I ended up making him more distant. Now we have no marriage at all. It is over before it had the chance to begin.'

Charlie lifted her chin and stared into her eyes. 'I love you and will support you no matter what happens.'

Her bottom lip quivered as fresh tears fell.

'My silly little sister. What am I to do with you?' He kissed the top of her head. 'Tell me, does Carleton know about the child?'

She shook her head, her throat too tight to speak.

'Does he suspect?'

She closed her eyes and nodded.

'Then you must be honest with him. Tell him everything.'

Her eyes widened at the prospect. 'I cannot,' she croaked.

'You must and you will. No more secrets in this family. I cannot abide it.'

'He will have nothing to do with me once he knows.'

'How can that be worse than it is now?' Charlie stood and walked back to the fireplace. 'Ever since your return you have hardly seen the man. That is no way to live.' He took a deep breath. 'Do you want to be his wife? Do you love him at all?'

'Yes…'

'Are you sure about that?'

She fumbled in her pocket for a handkerchief, and once found, blew her nose. Yes. She loved Carleton. In fact, she was surprised by just how much she missed him. But his change in behaviour frightened her. Gone was the attentive, dashing man she'd fallen in love with. Instead, he'd become stern and unapproachable within days of leaving England. How could she live with a man who no longer had kindness in his eyes?

'Tell me about it, Bella. Perhaps I can help in some way. I'm not going to be here forever. I'll be no use to you in the grave.'

She gave a sob and wiped her eyes. 'Don't talk like that. I cannot stand it.'

'I've failed Eden. I'm not going to fail you too. Now start from the beginning.'

~ ~ ~

Joel rested his body against the ship's rail, bracing himself for the slightest pain in his shoulder. With one arm in a sling tucked beneath his uniform jacket, he was careful to keep out of the way of people. The slightest touch could have him sweating in pain. The sea breeze lifted the hair on his forehead and neck, cooling him slightly. He needed a haircut, but he'd wait until he'd reach England before attending to that.

Below him on the deck, he watched the crowds scurrying about like ants. Soldiers, nurses, travellers, ship crew, dock workers all hurried back and forth. Behind him, from within the ship, came the noise of eager travellers settling in for their ocean journey.

He stared out into the distance, where Table Mountain dominated the view. He was sad to be leaving Africa. He'd come to think of it as home in a way. The sights and sounds, the heat and people were familiar now. Of course, nothing competed against Bradbury Hall, but he'd been in Africa for seven years. It was a long time. The army had replaced his family. He'd learnt to rely on his fellow officers to ease the loneliness, and at first it had worked well. The adventure and excitement kept his mind from thinking of home. But lately, for the last year and a half, a yearning to return home had claimed him and not let go.

The ships funnels belched smoke and the boarding siren wailed. Under his feet he felt the deck shudder as the enormous engines surged with power. Anticipation welled. He was going home. Despite the ache in his shoulder, he smiled. Time to start a new phase of his life. Time to reaffirm the links with his family, the estate, old friends, and... Eden.

He was conscious of the changes awaiting him back home. Much had happened in his absence. Not long after he joined the regiment, his mother died. That had been a blow, but on the whole, he had managed to keep the family and home intact in his mind. When he'd left England, his father had been alive, Charlie well, Annabella cheeky, pretty, I and Eden... Eden had been beautiful, a free spirit of the woodland where she lived.

What awaited him now?

The ship eased from its berth and glided out into the harbour. The breeze sharpened and Joel turned away from the rail. He glanced at a crippled solider standing near the door leading into one of the saloons. The soldier swayed on his crutches; one leg gone in battle.

'Major Bradbury?'

Joel checked his step and hurried over to steady the man with his good arm.

'Thanks, Sir.' The solider smiled.

'Stevens, isn't it?' Joel mused, helping the man to lean against a wall and out of the way of other passengers.

'Stevenson, Sir, Corporal Dave Stevenson.' He leaned against the support and breathed out slowly. 'I still haven't got the hang of these things yet.' He held up the crutches.

Joel grinned. 'I think it might be an art that takes practice, Corporal.'

Dave took of his hat and wiped the seat off from his forehead, his fair hair stuck to his head. 'Do you mind, Sir, if I sit down? This leg isn't used to holding all the weight and gets a bit shaky, like.'

'Of course, man, sit.' Joel again aided Stevenson in lowering to the deck. There were no chairs about and after a moment's hesitation, Joel join him and gently eased his backside down, careful not to jar his shoulder. 'We should have gone inside, it would be more comfortable.'

'Sorry, Sir, but I'm no sailor. Once inside my stomach has a mind of its own. I'm better out here.'

'Well, I'll keep you company for a while until dinner is announced. My stomach is the opposite of yours. Once on the ocean I'm always ravenous. I do nothing but eat.'

'You might struggle with a knife and fork, using only one hand.'

Joel chuckled. 'Yes, true. So far I've had only soup and sandwiches.'

Stevenson laid his crutches beside his good leg and gazed out through the iron rail. 'So, we're going back home to England. I've been away three years. I should be happy to be going back, but I'm not as excited as I should be, I don't think.'

'It affects men in different ways.'

'If you don't mind me asking, Sir, how do you feel? Was your clipped wing the reason for you to go home?'

'Yes. My shoulder stopped a bullet.' He glanced down at his padded and bandaged left shoulder.

'Normally they'd take it out and I'd be back in the mix of things, but this Boer bullet went in at an angle and wedge itself deep. The surgeon managed to get it out, but he wasn't sure what damaged had been done. Only once the swelling has gone down and the soreness gone, will I know what strength remains in the arm.'

'Does your family know about it yet?'

'No, not yet. It didn't seem worth writing when I was going home anyway. What about your family?'

'Oh aye, they know. I've been in hospital a while, long enough for letters to go back and forth.' Stevenson bent up his leg and rested his elbow on it. 'They say they don't care if I come home missing a leg, as long as I'm coming home to them. I'm an only child see, and I used to help my father run our grocers' shop.'

'Will you do that again?'

'I guess so. Funny how things change, isn't it? I hated working in that shop as a lad. All my friends would be out playing football or cricket and I'd be stuck behind a counter. The first opportunity I got to leave I took, and that was the army.' He tapped the toe of his boot on the deck. 'Now, I can't wait to get back there. I miss me mam and dad, and me gran, who lives with us. My mam makes the best jam roly-poly you've ever tasted. Dad brews his own beer in the back shed and Gran used to be my partner in cards.'

'There's nothing better in this world than returning home to a family that loves you.' A picture came into Joel's mind of the estate in autumn, the tall graceful trees, their leaves turning gold and amber, the squirrels scurrying around in the wood, collecting the last of their booty, harvest time and bringing in the hay, the smell of open fires as the gardeners raked up and burnt the fallen leaves.

He leaned his head back and smiled in remembrance. 'I long to go riding with my brother. We used to ride for miles. Sometimes we'd stop at a pub and have an ale and a hot pie smothered in gravy.'

'Me mam has written of a neighbour's daughter, Vera, who she hopes I'll one day marry. I'm not so sure what Vera has to say about it though. We got along all right before I went away, but…well, I'm not as I once was.'

'If this Vera is a decent woman, she'll not mind.'

'Maybe.' Stevenson lifted his face to the breeze. 'Will you have a girl waiting for you at home, Sir?'

Joel's stomach clenched. 'Perhaps. I'm ready for a family. However, I've been away longer than you, and I'm not sure what to expect when I arrive home.'

'None of us are, Sir, none of us are.'

A group of children ran by, the shoes thundering on the timber deck. One cheeky boy paused and waved to Joel and Stevenson before scampering off again. A harassed nanny tried to catch up as she wheeled a pram after them. Joel watched until they turned a corner at the bow of the ship and were out of sight. His heart constricted, thinking of the boy's lively face. A son. He wanted a son so badly it hurt. A boy to teach all the things his father taught him, to hunt, to fish, to ride, to play sports. He thought of Charlie. Two sons perhaps. Two fine boys to grow up together like he and Charlie did.

Emotion clogged his throat and he coughed to clear it. He'd been away from home too long…

~ ~ ~

Eden closed the oven door with her backside as she turned to the table and placed the tray of hot jam tarts down. At the other end of the table, Josephine read aloud from the morning's newspaper and Lillie sat beside her, drawing on a small chalkboard. Eden worried they'd be missing out on their education, and so each day she made them read and do simple sums. It was the best she could do for the moment. She'd been at Prim's Lodging House for five weeks now and it was getting harder for her to explain to the girls why they still lived there. To begin with, Bea's illness had lingered, giving Eden a good excuse to stay, but now Bea was up and about again, the girls cried to go home. They missed their grandfather, the cottage, the woods and school.

Using the back of her floured hand to wipe her hair from her eyes, Eden sighed then smiled at Josephine, encouraging her to continue when she stumbled over a word. 'You're reading very well, darling.'

Laurence came in through the back door, his usual smile in place. 'It's me.'

'As we can see.' Eden chuckled. Laurence, although exasperating at times, was such a sweet simple soul that she and the girls adored him. However, he was banned from shopping. Ever since that first morning when she gave him money to buy breakfast and he'd returned with only eggs, he'd shown that shopping for more than one item was beyond him. Now she either went with him or sent Josephine along.

Bea stepped down into the kitchen from the hallway. 'Did you hang those bed sheets out properly, Laurie?'

'Yes, Ma.'

'Emptied the copper?'

'Yes, Ma.'

'Brought in the coal?'

154

'Yes, Ma.'

Bea nodded and graced him with a small smile. 'Good boy. Now you may go to the river.'

Laurie whooped and dashed out the back door again.

Eden knew from experience that they'd not see him again until dark. The River Ouse that snaked through the centre of town, was his favourite place and on Sundays, she and the girls went with him and he would show them the banks he sat on, the boatmen he waved to, and anything else that caught his imagination.

'They look good, Eden.' Bea waved at the jam tarts. 'Will go a treat at afternoon tea.' She took her shawl off the hook on the back door. 'Will you be all right while I go and pay some accounts? I'll get the fresh fish from the market while I'm out, too. We'll have that later. Mr Rogers always likes a bit of fish on a Friday.'

Eden nodded and privately believed that their lodger of two weeks, Mr Rogers was too demanding. 'Yes, I'll be fine. I've an apple pie left in the oven, and then I'll do some ironing.'

'Nay, don't do too much.' Bea pinned on her hat and looked fondly at Lillie. 'Perhaps the girls might want to come with me? It's a lovely day for a walk.'

Eden raised her eyebrows at the girls, and Lillie jumped off her chair while Josephine shook her head.

'Well, little one, it's you and me then.' Bea rarely smiled, and only fully smiled at Lillie, who'd become her favourite. With everyone else she was strict and forthright, though never unkind. Bea Prim was a loner, used words sparingly and found fault easily. Yet, under that sharp composure, Eden sensed a fragileness about her.

In the five weeks she'd been at the lodgings, Bea hadn't spoken of her past or asked about Eden's. They worked and lived together in quiet harmony. For how long Eden stayed there, would depend on Bea needing her. Since recovering from her illness, she'd not mentioned about Eden leaving, and so Eden took each day as it came, happy she had a roof over her and the girls' head and that for now, they were safe from Clifton.

She'd made sure she didn't venture out too much, and only a few of their neighbours knew her name. Thankfully, Bea's lack of interest in socialising within the neighbourhood meant Eden could stay away from prying eyes and gossip. With so many lodgers coming and going, one more stranger in their midst didn't cause too much speculation.

After Bea and Lillie had gone, Josephine slid off her chair and came to stand nearer to Eden. 'Mam?'

'Hmm?' Using a knife, she started slipping the tarts out of the baking tray moulds and onto a wire rack to cool.

'Why can't we go home?'

Her knife hovered mid-air as Eden gazed at Josephine. 'We will, one day.'

'Why hasn't Grandfather come yet? You sent him a letter weeks ago.'

Eden continued placing the tarts on the rack. Twelve days ago, she had sent Grandfather a letter telling him she and the girls were well and staying in lodgings. She'd not put the address on that first letter in case it fell into wrong hands. Clifton's threat was too raw for her to lower her guard, but eventually she'd send Grandfather their details so he could visit them. She silently prayed he was well. 'He's likely busy, now the weather's nice.'

Josephine's expression turned mutinous. 'Uncle Charlie said he'd teach me to ride a pony this summer. I *want* to go home.'

'I thought you liked it here?'

'I'd rather be home. Please, Mam, *please* can we go?'

'Not yet.'

'Why?'

'Because I said so.' Sighing, Eden grabbed an oven cloth and opened the oven door to check the pie. 'Now, help me get the clothes out for ironing.'

'No.'

Eden shut the oven door and raised one eyebrow at her. 'Pardon?'

'No, I won't help you.'

'Don't you dare speak to me like that, Miss. Now, go get the clothes or you'll find yourself in bed without supper.'

'You ruin everything!'

Eden blinked in shock, of late Josephine's wilful nature had been subdued because of their new environment, but as she stared at the stubborn tilt of her daughter's chin, anger simmered. 'You will do as you're told, young lady, or feel the back of my hand.'

'I wish you had died and not my Da.'

Eden gasped. 'You spoilt little girl, what a horrid thing to say.'

'You're mean and I *hate* you!' Josephine raced from the kitchen, along the back yard and disappeared out into the cut.

'Josephine!' Eden called her, but knew it was useless. Her daughter's temper would have to cool before she listened to reason. 'Damn. Blast.'

In a fit of frustration, Eden brought the pie out of the over and slammed it onto the table, then after taking off her apron, she strode outside and down the cut to the street. Looking both ways, she couldn't see Josephine and cursed again. The girls often played in the cut with other children from the street, but today it was deathly quiet, all the children being at the local school. She would send the girls to school come Monday. They had too much time to waste and Josephine needed no help in becoming unruly.

Mrs Henderson, a basket over her arm, came out of her front door and closed it behind her. 'Good day, Mrs Harris.'

'How are you, Mrs Henderson?'

'Well, thank you. I'm just off to the shops. Never stops, does it?'

'No.' Eden smiled. 'If you see my Josephine, would you send her home for me?'

'Of course. I usually see her around the corner looking in Mr Abbott's sweet shop window.'

'Thanks.'

Mrs Henderson hesitated. 'You should think about putting her in school. The authorities will be knocking on your door, if you don't.'

'I-I haven't made up my mind whether we'll stay long here long term as yet.'

'Oh?' The other woman inched closer. 'Will you be returning home then, from where you came?'

'From Manchester? No, we won't be returning there.' Eden stepped back, hating having to lie and surprised at how quickly the lies sprang to her tongue.

'Manchester is it?' Mrs Henderson frowned. 'I thought Josephine told me you used to live in the country, some place near Skipton...I can't remember the village name now.'

Annoyed, Eden crossed her arms. Likely this stupid woman had been pumping the girls for all sorts of information titbits. 'Well, good day. I've ironing to do.'

'Good day. And I'll send Josephine home if I see her.'

'Don't worry about it. She's likely gone to the river with Laurence.' Eden nodded and turned back the way she came. She didn't need nosy women like Henderson spreading gossip. She'd have to curtail Josephine's freedom. Maybe she would settle down if Grandfather came to stay for a while.

Yes, she'd write to him again, today, and tell him their address and ask him to visit them as soon as he could. She rubbed her forehead, weary of wondering if she'd done the right thing. Had there been an alternative? Josephine wasn't the only one to miss home. There was an ache inside her chest she couldn't get rid of either. She missed Nathan, Grandfather, home. She was tired of being strong and of worrying. When would it all end?

Chapter 14

Clifton sat on the chair and thumped his walking cane on the floor between his knees. 'Now listen here, Miller. I don't appreciate having to chase you for news.'

Miller leaned back in his chair on the other side of the desk. 'Mr Clifton, I have reported my findings so far.'

'But you've stopped searching for her! We know she went to York, but the trail could have gone cold now. Why aren't you working on it?'

'Because your money has run out, sir. The agreed price has taken me so far, but I can do no more until I receive more money.'

Anger boiled in his chest. 'You want to rob me blind, more like. I'll give you no more money until you come up with new evidence of her whereabouts.'

Miller shook his head, laying his hands out flat. 'I can do no more.'

Frustration added to the anger and blood suffused his face as it always did when he was close to a rage. 'I need her found!'

'And I must pay my bills.'

Clifton strove for patience, hoping the cunning investigator opposite would do a deal. 'Now, Miller, surely we can come to some agreement? We are reasonable men and I've paid you handsomely before and will do so again.'

Miller sat forward, resting his elbows on the paperwork covering his desk. 'Mr Clifton, you were referred to me because of my good reputation to achieve results. The men who referred me are my clients, men I hold many secrets for. As well as investigating for them, I also investigate the client.' He smiled. 'I want to make sure I will receive all my payment and not delve into something that may ruin my business, if you understand my meaning. I have no wish to put the police offside. So, as you can see, I am thorough in everything. I do not need your custom, nor do I need to work for you especially since I found out of your circumstances.' Miller leaned back with another satisfied smile.

A cold shiver of fear ran down Clifton's spine. 'You know nothing about me.'

Miller shifted some papers on his desk and found the one he was looking for. 'You were born to Ada and Leonard Clifton. Your mother is sister to the late Colonel Bradbury, and your father was a gambler and died with debts that had to be paid by the Colonel, this he had done many times throughout his sister's marriage to save your father from going to debtors prison.'

'Shut up! Shut your mouth!' Pain squeezed his chest and he had to brace a hand against the desk to draw air into his lungs. The bastard, *bastard!* With his eyes he begged Miller to stop, but he continued.

'Since your father's untimely death, something which has never been solved, your uncle, the Colonel, has financed you and your mother to live comfortably within your society. However, recent developments have seen you ostracized from the family and you no

161

longer have the Bradbury money.' Miller dropped the sheet of paper with a look of disgust. 'So, tell me, Mr Clifton, how do you propose to pay me for my services?'

Fighting for every breath of air, Clifton rose shakily to his feet and stumbled to the door. The pain in his left arm and shoulder nearly brought him to his knees. A vice was squeezing his chest. At the door, he paused and glanced back. 'I'll see you...in Hell, Mr Miller.'

'Undoubtedly, Mr Clifton.' He smiled. 'Good day.'

Somehow, he managed to get down the staircase from Miller's office and out onto the street again. He leant against the building, closed his eyes and took deep breaths. The noise of the busy south London street faded while he concentrated on easing the tightness in his chest. It took several minutes before he could open his eyes and focus on his surroundings. A sharp breeze whistled down the street, sending whirls of paper and rubbish before it. An ache lingered, resounding through his body as though he'd been hit by a dozen trampling horses.

He pushed away from the wall and leaning heavily on his cane walked to the end of the street and hailed a passing cab to take him to his gentlemen's club in Belgravia. For the journey he sat with his eyes closed, feeling nauseous and depressed. Blasted Miller. It was all his fault. Why did he have to bring up his father, for God's sake? Leonard Clifton had no place in his life, never had done. The man had been a waster, and he'd been the one mistake of his mother's life.

When the cab pulled to a stop outside the impressive white stone building, he gingerly climbed down and paid his fare. A few hours in the quiet peace of his club would soothe him, and a glass of two of brandy would be exactly what he needed. After ascending the five stone steps to the door, he paused to rest. The gleaming black doors opened and Norbert, the doorman frowned at him as he entered the entrance hall. He ignored Norbert and sniffed appreciatively of the club's unique scent of cigars, brandy, bee's wax polished wood. Wealth seemed to ooze out of papered walls, seep from the thick carpet. Only in this place did he feel truly at home and comfortable.

He started for the staircase that led up to the next floor, knowing he'd find some friendly faces around a billiard table or in the snug, book-lined library.

'Er, Mr Clifton...' Norbert's tone, brought him up short, and he realised he'd hadn't given him his hat and cane.

'Sorry, my good fellow, my mind isn't my own today.' He removed his hat and offered it to Norbert, who stood dithering.

'I'm sorry, My Clifton, but I cannot admit you today.'

'Pardon?' Confused, Clifton frowned and rubbed his forehead. If he didn't sit down soon, he'd fall down and cause a spectacle.

'Please, wait here while I fetch Mr Solomon.'

With a groan, he sat down on an occasional chair by the window overlooking the street while Norbert hurried off. He was starting to feel a little better.

'Clifton, old fellow, surprised to see you here.' Johnny Radcliff greeted him with a handshake and a grin. 'I knew you'd come out of it somehow. Didn't quite believe it at first. Some mistake was it?'

He stood and shook his hand, not having a clue what the man was on about. What was wrong with him today? 'I don't know—'

'Mortimer can't be trusted. He gossips worse than an old woman.'

'Listen, Johnny, you couldn't lend me a hundred pounds, could you?'

Radcliff frowned. 'Er…'

'Fifty then? You know I'm good for it.'

'Sorry, old pal, but I'm cleaned out. Had a bad night at the tables, you know how it is.'

'Mr Clifton!' Solomon, the manager of the club, swiftly crossed the carpet with two lackeys close on his heels. In one smooth action, he propelled him towards the doorway. 'I do apologise, but unfortunately you are denied entry.'

Enraged by the manhandling, Clifton pulled his arm out of Solomon's grasp. 'I beg your pardon? What is the meaning of this?'

Solomon stood erect and without expression. 'You are denied entry.'

'On what grounds?'

'Unpaid membership and unsuitable behaviour becoming of a gentleman.'

'Are you insane?'

'Not in the least, Mr Clifton. Now, please vacate the premises.'

'I certainly will not! This is outrageous.' Had the world gone mad today or just him? First, he'd been denied credit at his tailors until his account was paid, his tobacconist had done the same, then the unsatisfactory appointment with Miller and now this.

'I assure you my information is correct, sir.'

He banged his cane down. 'On whose authority is this?'

'Charles Bradbury, sir, your cousin.'

As though someone had thrown a bucket of ice water over him, Clifton staggered. No… Please God, no. He backed away from them, a small crowd of men had gathered, all coming to watch his humiliation. His throat and mouth dry, he couldn't speak in his defence. Radcliff, Mortimer, Johnstone, Rollings, they were all staring, eager to see his downfall. Like father like son, they'd say.

In an instant, something snapped in his brain. He straightened, pasted on a smile and, fighting the urge to retch, glared at them. 'Ah, some ridiculous mistake, I'm sure. Charlie's not well. Quite ill, in fact. He's made a mistake.' He nodded to them all in general, feigning light heartedness. 'Cherrio, my good fellows and Radcliff, stay away from those tables.' He grinned as though his life depended on it and jauntily left the club and walked down the steps. Only once on the street did he drop the act. Inside his chest tightened again but not with pain just a cold, rock-hard knot of fury.

His whole life had been overshadowed by the Bradburys. They had money, prestige, a secure place in society, beautiful homes and charming good looks. And he was the poor cousin. The one who could never achieve the same heights as they did, he could never be one of them.

How long would he suffer because of them, his saintly cousins? Charlie thought to cut him off without a penny, did he? 'Well, we'll see about that.'

Tapping his cane against his boot, he looked up the street for a cab. The Bradbury's thought they could make him suffer because of his treatment of Eden, did they? He laughed deep in his throat. His laying with her will be nothing compared to what he had install for Eden and little Josephine now. And they had no one to blame but themselves. They drove him to such evils. If they'd accepted him as an equal none of this would have happened. Yet, now there was no going back.

He hailed a cab and waited for it to slow down in front of him. As he climbed into the dark interior, he smiled. None of this was his fault and they would all pay dearly. He may not be a Bradbury, but they'd learn he wasn't to be ignored either.

~ ~ ~

As the hired carriage rumbled through the open gates, Joel stuck his head out the window. 'Stop here!'

The driver slowed the horses and Joel climbed down as pre-arranged. Now, standing on the driveway, emotion rose. His eyes smarted and he blinked rapidly. Grown men didn't cry. *Majors* didn't cry!

'Shall I continue to the house, Major Bradbury?'

Joel shook his head. 'No, give me a few minutes.' He wanted to see the Hall without interruption.

Straightening his uniform jacket over his arm sling, he took a deep breath and walked up the drive. Rounding the bend, Bradbury Hall came into view and he stared at it, not bothering to blink away the tears that gathered. He was home.

The warm weather of late spring brought the flowers out into bloom, insects hovered lazily, and the very tops of the trees swayed in a breeze not felt on the ground. On the far side of the front garden, a gardener wheeled a barrow.

Joel wiped his eyes and continued walking. The fine gravel crunched beneath his feet, but apart from the odd call of a bird in the woodland, it was the only sound. At the front step of the house, he paused and raised his face to the sun. A sudden calmness overwhelmed him, scattering away his nervousness. He'd waited for this moment for so long. It was hard for him to truly believe he was here.

He hesitated only a moment, before stepping forward and opening the door. The scent of polish and fresh flowers filled his nose, while the coolness of the house contrasted to the warmth outside. He stood and listened. The longcase clock ticked solemnly, as though it was frightened to be too loud. He looked up the staircase at the portraits of the deceased family members and sighed when he came to his father's. Both parents gone and he wasn't here to witness it.

Joel winced as his boots clicked against the polished timber floorboards as he walked into the drawing room. He hadn't sent word of his arrival, wanting to surprise Charlie, and not having people waiting for his homecoming, gave him time to re-familiarise himself with the Hall. Memories crowded his mind. He touched the wing-backed chair his father favoured whenever he sat in this room. The beauty of his mother smiled down at him from a portrait on the wall between the two windows.

Footsteps sounded from the hallway and he turned as Mellors entered the room.

'What the...' Mellors checked his stride, his eyes widened when recognition dawned. 'Master Joel?'

'The very same.' Joel grinned, his heart brimming. 'How are you, Mellors?' He stepped forward eagerly to shake the other man's hand.

'Why, Major, you sent no word!' Mellors pumped Joel's hand up and down. 'We had no idea, sir, no idea.'

Joel winced as the enthusiastic motion jarred his shoulder 'I wanted to surprise you all.'

'That you did, sir, that you did.' Mellors finally dropped his hand and turned for the door just as the carriage arrived at the house. 'I'll have your luggage sent up and will inform Master Charlie, he'll—'

'No, Mellors, let me go. Where is he?'

'He's sitting out on the back terrace, sir, enjoying the warmth.'

'How is he?'

Mellors smiled. 'He'll be much better now you're home, that I do know.'

Joel nodded and headed out into the hallway, He crossed to the front parlour and out into the conservatory where he paused and thought of his mother who'd died while he was in Africa. She loved her glassy leafed plants. He touched the leaves of one huge palm that filled the corner of the glassed room.

A dog barked, drawing his attention outside. A cocker spaniel raced across the lower terrace after a red ball. On the far right of the terrace, Charlie sat in one of two large wicker chair, a blanket over his knees. Joel watched his brother, his eyes filling again as the sight of Charlie throwing the ball for the dog.

For the first time, the reality hit. Charlie was sick. From this distance he looked an old man with the rug about his lap. His skin goose bumped. He couldn't lose another member of his family, not yet. *Let us have some years together before the hideous disease takes him.*

Striding across the lawn, Joel didn't want to waste another minute. 'What's this I see, you slacking your responsibilities again? Nothing ever changes.'

Charlie jerked in his seat and twisted around. 'Excuse me?'

Joel grinned and jogged to his brother.

'Lord, am I dreaming?' Charlie threw off the rug and rose. 'Is it really you?'

They came together in a tight hug. Joel closed his eyes at the frailness of his once strapping brother and held him tighter, ignoring the pain in his shoulder.

'I can't believe it.' Charlie stepped back and sniffed. 'You sent no word. I even had a letter posted to you yesterday!' Then he sobered and frowned at the sling poking out of the jacket. 'What happened?'

'A bullet. Not life threatening, but enough to get me home.' Joel cleared his throat and sniffed too. So much emotion in one day, he hadn't expected that. 'How is everyone?'

'Good. Annabella is with her husband today, although she still lives here for the moment and refuses to live at Carleton's home while ever his mother is in residence.'

'She never changes, does she?'

'Perhaps motherhood will.'

His eyes widened in surprise. 'A child for our Annabella. Imagine.' He grinned. 'We are to be uncles then.'

'So, it seems.' Charlie's smile didn't reach his eyes as he sat down.

Joel sat in the chair opposite and gazed at his brother. 'Is she happy with Carleton? I always liked the man and felt he was a good match for her, despite father's protests. Her letters sent on her honeymoon spoke much of the places she'd seen but not of herself.'

'Annabella is finding out that sometimes impulsive actions have repercussions. I'll fill you in later on that subject.'

Frowning, Joel fiddled with his empty sleeve pinned to his jacket. He hated being left out of things. Charlie seemed stiff and ill at ease. There was an air of disquiet about the place. He sighed. Had he honestly expected everything to be as it once was? Once more he gazed around the house and gardens, reaffirming the memories, the links, the love he felt for the estate.

'I am glad you're home.' Charlie smiled. 'Forgive my bad mood. I haven't been sleeping well.'

'It's good to be home. A little strange, but good all the same.'

'You're long overdue.'

'Yes, but there was a war on.'

'Not only in Africa either.' Charlie glanced at Mellors crossing the lawn carrying a tea tray. 'You read my mind, Mellors.'

'As I've told you before, it's my job, Master Charlie.' He smiled and placed the tray on the small wrought iron table next to the chairs. Pouring out the tea, Mellors looked at Joel. 'I'm having your room aired and readied, Sir. I'll personally unpack your luggage.'

'Thank you.' Joel took his teacup, leaving the saucer behind, and reclined back, sipping the brew. Once Mellors departed, Joel studied his brother, noticing the pallor of his skin, the shadows bruising under his eyes. Charlie's hair had thinned and started to recede. Was his health the battle he referred to just now?

'I am much changed, yes?' Charlie gave a wry smile and patted the dog panting next to his chair.

'I think we all have.'

'Some more than others.'

Joel stared out over the gardens towards the stables and the woodland beyond. Where was she? 'I've missed so much. You've had to shoulder the burden and I'm sorry for that. But now I'm home again, I don't want you thinking I'll push you aside and do everything my way. I want this to be a partnership.'

'To be honest, Joel, I don't want to do it anymore. I'm tired. The estate is yours. It is all yours. I only want to live the remaining years left to me in simple happiness.'

He looked at Charlie, at the weariness in his eyes. He'd seen death and dying men too many times and wasn't going to argue with Charlie or say that he would live to be an old man. They both knew the opposite. 'Then simple pleasures are all you'll have. I promise. We'll go riding and fishing and do all the things we did before.'

'It seems a lifetime ago when we were all together and happy.' Charlie stirred his tea. 'Much has happened. I don't know where to begin.'

'I know there is a lot for me to learn about the last seven years, but your letters have helped keep the ties with home strong.'

Charlie bowed his head. 'I didn't do a good job of it, Joel. I didn't take care of them as I should have.'

'What do you mean?'

'Father, Mother, Annabella, Eden... I feel responsible.'

'Don't talk nonsense. You did what you could do. Mother had cancer, Father had pneumonia, and so Annabella married a man father didn't really approve of, what does it matter now? She has always been wilful...' His words dried up as Eden came to mind.

'There's much you don't know.'

'Naturally.' Did she ever think of him?

Charlie placed his teacup back on the table, untouched. 'What are your plans now you're home?'

'That largely depends on my shoulder.'

'The estate needs you. I can't give it the attention it needs. Some days I haven't the energy to get out of bed and in winter I'm practically housebound.'

'We'll work it together with me taking the bulk of the burden.' Joel smiled.

'No.' Charlie straightened. 'I've had enough of worries, of responsibilities. It's your turn now. You must deal with it.'

'Of course. I didn't mean—'

'I've turned cousin Clifton out of the family without a penny.'

Joel stared and carefully put his teacup alongside Charlie's. The hairs on the back of his neck stood on end. Something was wrong, very wrong. 'Tell me.'

Charlie rubbed his forehead. 'There's no easy way to say this.'

'So, say it and get it over with.'

'Clifton raped Eden. Josephine is his child.'

The words ricocheted around his brain but refused to have meaning. Clifton raped Eden. Josephine is his child. Around and around the words went, taunting him, stabbing him. He griped the arm of the wicker chair. He found it hard to breathe. His darling girl... *The bastard!*

'Joel. Joel?'

Dazed he stared at Charlie, who bent over him, had a worried look in his eyes.

'I'm sorry Joel, I shouldn't have said it like that.' Charlie turned and yelled for Mellors.

Joel covered his face with one hand. His stomach churned; bile rose.

'Mellors!' Charlie patted Joel's back. 'You need a brandy. I'm sorry Joel, really sorry.'

Joel was vaguely aware of Mellors rushing out onto the lawn only to return inside again and come back with two brandies on a silver tray. Joel threw the first brandy down the back of his throat, needing the fire to burn into him, to sear away the knowledge received. The second brandy helped him to focus, to think, to feel. 'I will kill him.'

'No!' Charlie sat in the chair and faced him. 'No, you're not going to jail for him. I won't lose you a second time. We'll involve the police if we have to. He's raped maids, too. They may testify against him.'

'I will kill him, Charlie.'

'Joel, listen to me—'

He jerked to his feet, his blood throbbing through him, his heart beating against his ribs. How many Boers, men defending what they believed in, had he killed? Men who had wives and children. He had killed men because the word 'war' had been above their heads, because he'd been trained to do it without thought, had been expected to do it. Yet, all that time, one man, a monster, had done depraved things within *his* own home and had gone unpunished. Where was the justice?

A wild rage threatened his reason. He kicked the table over, shattering the tea service and brandy glasses across the grass. The dog yelped and ran behind Charlie's chair. Joel swore violently, saying every filthy word he knew and doubling up often. In his frenzy, he kicked at his chair awkwardly, the result causing his shoulder to jar. Pain tore his breath away. He crouched on the grass, using his good arm to brace himself and sucked in air.

'Joel.'

He slowly turned and looked at Charlie, whose expression reflected the hurt twisting his gut. 'God, Charlie. Eden...'

'I know.'

Mellors tread gently towards him and helped him up. 'Come inside, Sir.'

Joel turned to Charlie. 'Why didn't you tell me?'

173

'I haven't known long myself.' He ran his hand through his hair. 'It's such a mess. Come inside and I'll fill you in.'

'I love her.' There, he'd finally said it aloud after all these years.

'I gathered as much.'

'I have always loved her.' His eyes stung with unshed tears. He swallowed several times to ease the constriction in his throat. 'I should have stayed, defied father, and remained home to protect her.'

'We can't turn back time. You always knew you would serve sometime in the military, father wanted it, expected it. Besides, how were we to know Clifton would do that to her.'

His stomach churned again at the thought. 'Was…was Nathan, her husband, a good man?'

Charlie gave a small smile. 'Adored her, he did. He met his death through Clifton. If he'd stayed away from them, Nathan wouldn't have gone into that swollen river.'

'Where is she?'

'Gone. Clifton threatened her once too often, especially when he found out Josephine was his. So she left one day without telling anyone and has gone into hiding.'

'Not even her grandfather knows where she is?'

'No. Though he says she'll contact him once she's settled, but we don't know when that might be or whether she'll risk giving him her address.'

'Have you tried to find her?'

'Yes. I have a man, Mr Cole, working on it now. He believes she's gone to York by train. The stationmaster recognised her. Cole's searching York as we speak.'

'Then that's where I'll go too.' He started towards the house.

'Wait.' Charlie caught up with him and they walked into the house together. 'He's coming in the morning with the latest update. You'd have a better chance finding her and the girls with more information. Besides, after all your travelling, you need a decent meal and a good night's rest.'

'I won't be able to rest now, Charlie.'

'And you'll do no good going off half crazy, will it? You know I'm right. Plus, Annabella will be home soon. You can't leave without seeing her.'

'I suppose.' Joel sighed. The thought of Eden out there alone with the girls, perhaps frightened, homeless, without friends or help broke his heart in two. He had to find her.

Chapter 15

Horatio lent on his stick, a long tomato stake, and bent down to pull out a weed from the vegetable bed. Speckled hens cackled around him, eager to peck at the grubs and bugs he disturbed as he gardened. The sun was warm on his back, a back that now ached after an hour tidying up the garden, planting seeds and raking manure into the soil.

He looked at his dirt grained hands. He'd have to wash soon, as Barney was coming over for a chat and to share a bottle of ale. Since Eden's departure, Barney had taken it upon himself to call in every evening to check on him. Horatio smiled. Barney's visits were the highlight of his day. The cottage was lonely without the girls and, for the first time in his long life, Horatio was living alone.

He patted the folded letter in his shirt pocket; Eden's invitation for him to visit her and the girls at their lodgings. He wanted to go, and planned to, but first he'd see Master Charlie and let him know. With luck, Charlie might offer to go with him, and they could go in his carriage, which would be far better than a rattling noisy train full of strangers. He sighed. Despite wanting to see his girls, the thought of travelling to York didn't please him. He was too old to go gallivanting about and his legs wouldn't carry him far.

Secretly, he'd hoped Eden would come home to visit him, even for just a day, but he was being self-ish. Although Clifton had been banished from the estate, they couldn't risk her coming home.

A bang came from within the cottage. He glanced over his shoulder to the back door. His hearing wasn't that good at the best of times. A wood pidgin cooed from a tree behind the woodshed and Horatio yawned. The warm weather and day's toil left him tired. An afternoon nap before Barney arrived was in order, and then he may even go to the pub for a quiet pint. Earnshaw often gave him a lift home again or let him sleep in one of his spare beds.

Noise came from the cottage again, louder this time. Horatio shuffled along the narrow paths between the vegetable beds to the back door. Had he left the kettle on the hob? Had a bird flown in? Not for the first time, he thought of getting a dog. It would keep him company and let him know if anyone was about at night. Poachers often snatched on of his hens if they didn't manage to grab some game.

At the back door, the sound of scuffling made him pause and wait for his eyes to adjust to the dimness inside. At the far end of the cottage near the front door a person had his back to him. Silently, Horatio took a few more steps. He glanced at the kitchen knife on the table. No, he wasn't using that. He didn't want to end his life locked away in a cell. 'Can I help you?'

The stranger swung around startled. Clifton. 'Ah, old man. I didn't notice you there.'

Horatio looked at the mess Clifton had made on the dresser. 'Too busy going through my things, hey?'

A sly smile changed Clifton's features into an evil mask. 'Well, now you're here I won't have to search any more, will I?'

'Whatever it is. I don't have it, or if I do, I won't part with it. So, get along with you.'

'I'll be gone when I'm ready.' Clifton gazed about the sitting room and kitchen, then at the ladder to the loft. 'Has she been in contact with you yet?'

'No.'

'I don't believe you.' From the mantelpiece, Clifton picked up a small portrait of Eden's mother. 'I'm not leaving until I have what I came here for.'

'I have nothing you want.'

'My dear fellow, do you honestly think I am a simpleton?'

Horatio gripped the garden stake tighter. 'A simpleton? No. Evil baggage that needs horsewhipping, yes.'

Clifton's small eyes narrowed into slits; his lips twisted in a cruel grimace. 'You won't stand in my way.' With a swipe of his ham fist, he sent the contents of the dresser onto the floor.

His heart thudded in his chest as he looked at the broken plates his wife had collected over the years, they, and her embroidered handkerchiefs were all he had left of her since she died twelve years ago. Slowly he raised his gaze from the mess on the floor to Clifton's puffy red face. 'Smash it all. What do I care? But you'll never get a word of her whereabouts from me.'

Clifton strode across the destruction, china breaking beneath his boots. He stopped within a foot of Horatio and glared. 'If you don't give me her address, I'll snap every bone in your body.'

'You don't frighten me. I remember you as a mean little boy who grew into a mean man masquerading as a gentleman.'

His reactions were too slow to avoid the back-hander Clifton gave him. He stumbled back against the kitchen table and held onto it one handed, using the other hand to raise the stake to ward off another hit. Stars danced before his eyes.

'Where is she, old man? You know and you're going to tell me.'

'You think I'm senile?' Horatio tried to focus on the blurry figure, he blinked, but his sight remained unfocused. 'I'd rather die that let you anywhere near her.'

Clifton's fist into his stomach sent him crashing to his knees. His lungs wouldn't work. He gasped, reeling in pain. As though he weighed no more than a child, Clifton dragged him up again and smashed his fist into his face. For a moment everything went black. Horatio fell back against the table and then to the floor.

Pain was everything, everywhere. Clifton's boot struck his stomach, he used Horatio's own stake to whack him about the head and back. It seemed Hell had opened its gates and welcomed him, for nothing could ever be as bad as this. Vile curses and spittle flew about his head as Clifton's rage continued. There was no use trying to protect himself from the madman, his body had given up, his mind was slowly closing down.

Like a rag doll, Clifton grabbed him by the shirt to haul him up again, but his attention was drawn to the letter, now sticking out of his shirt pocket.

'Ah ha!' Clifton dropped him and grabbed the letter.

'No...' He couldn't breathe. Oh, blessed Lord...

'Thank you, my friend.' Clifton held the letter aloft, grinning widely. 'And hopefully you'll be dead before anyone finds you.'

Horatio, nearly blind, fought against the blackness wanting to overwhelm him as Clifton opened Eden's precious letter.

Clifton paused and looked around. 'Perhaps I should cover my tracks.'

Horatio's fragile hold on life slipped away when Clifton lit a match and put it to the papers littered about...

~ ~ ~

Joel paced the drawing room floor as Mellors showed Mr Cole out. He had to think. What would he do in Eden's place?

'So, what shall we do?' Annabella sat on a chair by the window, her silent husband standing behind her.

'Go to York, obviously.' Joel frowned.

Charlie, sitting on the sofa, crossed one leg over the other. 'Cole said he's door knocked on every door in a two-mile radius from the station. If she was still in the area, he'd have found her.'

'He hasn't searched every street, every house in York, Charlie,' he scoffed. 'He easily could have missed her.'

'What if she isn't in York?' Annabella sighed. 'What if she boarded another train or coach and has gone elsewhere? How will we ever find her then?'

He didn't want to think of that. 'Try to remember, Bella, did Eden mention, at any time, a place she'd like to go?'

'No, not that I can recall. She always loved being here.' She twisted her fingers in her lap. 'I cannot remember anywhere specific that she has mentioned.'

'This wasn't planned, Joel.' Charlie sighed. 'She left on impulse, to get away in a hurry. She would go to a city, to hide in the masses.'

Mellors returned and stood in the doorway expectantly. Joel nodded to him. 'Pack my things, please, and send the carriage around.'

'Yes, sir.'

'Pack mine too.' Charlie stood and faced Joel. 'I'm not staying behind this time.'

Joel placed his hand on Charlie's shoulder. 'Good. Thank you.'

Annabella rose in a huff. 'You both aren't leaving me behind! Mellors, have my maid pack for me too.'

'Dearest,' Carleton caught her elbow, 'you can't possibly think to go?'

'I can and I will!' She glared at him with a questioning lift of her eyebrow. 'Will you accompany me, or do you have other more important business to attend to?'

He flushed but stood tall. 'I will go with you.'

Her stance softened slightly. 'Thank you.' She reached out her hand and held his. 'It's important to me.'

Carleton kissed her hand, his eyes full of love. 'Then it's important to me too.'

They all turned to the doorway again as Mellors rushed back in, his eyes wide. 'Masters, there's a fire reported. Barney says it's coming from Horatio Morely's cottage.'

Joel and Charlie looked at each other and then Joel sprang forward. 'Have the men brought out the fire barrel and pump?'

Mellors followed him and they hurried from the house. 'Yes, Major. Barney called for it straight away.'

There was an exodus of outdoor estate staff running across the field towards the wood. Even though running jarred his shoulder, Joel joined them and was soon in the cool shady wood. The smell of smoke grew stronger as they neared the cottage. Crackling flames could be heard but not yet seen.

On the front path, men were pumping the handle of the large water barrel upon on a flatbed wagon, built for the purpose of emergency fires. Shouts and yells came from a group of men beyond the pump and Joel pushed through the crowd to see better.

Barney stumbled out of the cottage door, dragging Horatio. Joel and two other men ran to help and together they lifted him and gently placed him on the grass. Behind them came a whoosh and the timber roof shingles caved in, allowing flames to roar up to the sky.

'Horatio!' Barney knelt and tapped the old man's sunken cheeks, but there was no response.

Joel bent and listened for a heartbeat and then turned his face to feel for any breath coming from Horatio's mouth. Nothing. 'He's gone.'

Barney rocked back, his mouth gaping denial.

The bruising on Horatio's face, the swollen eye and cut lip, drew Joel's attention. 'He's been bashed.'

'Sir, we should move away.' A groomsman came to stand beside him. 'We can't contain that fire. It's out of control.'

Nodding, Joel indicated for them to all withdraw, out of harm's way. The roof was engulfed with flames, smoke billowed out of the front door and seeped out of the cracks in the walls. He stared at the cottage, Eden's home, the one place, apart from the wood, which signified where she belonged.

'Joel!'

He turned and frowned on seeing Charlie, Annabella and Carleton walking up the woodland path. He stepped in front of Horatio's body to shield Annabella from it, but she cried and darted around him to kneel beside the old man.

'Oh, poor Grandfather.' She tenderly wiped his cheek, a tear slipping from her lashes. 'He was such a dear man.' Her hand hovered and she frowned. 'Why does he look…'

'He's been beaten, Bella,' Joel murmured.

Her hand flew to stifle another cry. 'Why? Why would anyone want to do this to him? He's old. He couldn't harm anyone?'

Charlie, having regained his breath from the walk, shook his head. 'Horatio beaten, the cottage ablaze. This was no accident.'

'No.' Carleton, his blue eyes full of concern, helped Annabella up and held her close to him. 'Let's return to the house. There's nothing we can do here now.'

Joel praised the men and told most of them to return back to work.

'Master?' Barney, shoulders bowed, came to look upon his old pal once more. 'May I have your permission to organise the undertaker? Horatio was a good friend.'

Joel rubbed his forehead in thought. 'Of course. Arrange the funeral and send all the bills to me. I'll leave it up to you. Make sure he has a good send off.' It was the least he could do for Eden. He turned away as Barney laid his own jacket over Horatio's face and joined his family for the walk home.

Once in the drawing room, they sat or stood in silence while Mellors poured them all a brandy. Carleton held Annabella's hand. 'I don't think you should go to York today. You should rest.'

'I'll be perfectly fine.' She gave him a small smile. 'Eden will need a woman with her when she hears about her grandfather. Lord, I miss her so...' She sipped her brandy and glanced at Joel. 'She's completely alone in the world now. Hasn't another living relative.'

'She has us.' Charlie threw back a large mouthful of the fiery liquid. 'She'll always have us. We are her family.'

Unable to keep still, Joel swallowed the last of his brandy and placed the glass down. Out the window, the carriage waited for them. 'Are we ready to go?'

~ ~ ~

Eden sat at the kitchen table chopping carrots and turnips. She glanced at Josephine, who refused to brush her hair and tie her boot laces. Scooping up a handful of vegetables, she plopped them into the stew pot that already held beef, stock and potatoes. 'You want to go to school looking like that, do you?'

'I don't care.' Josephine's expression was rebellious. 'I hate that school.'

'You hate everything.'

'I want to go to my old school. Why can't we go home to Grandfather?'

'We will, just not yet.'

'You're mean!'

She ignored the rude outburst. 'Just tidy yourself up, please.'

'No.'

Eden grabbed another carrot and started chopping. 'I'll not argue with you again. Go to school like that then, if it'll please you.'

Josephine's stance softened. 'Can I stay home and help you? I'll work all day, I promise. You need help now Mrs Prim is in bed again.'

'You have to go to school. It's the law.' More carrots went into the pot. 'Why must you cause a scene? Lillie goes off without a moments bother.'

'Lillie is a baby!'

Closing her eyes, Eden prayed for patience. 'Please, just go to school, Josephine. I haven't the energy to fight this morning.' She'd been up since before dawn to get a head start on the housework. She rose and placed the pot on the stove. 'Go get your sister, it's time to go. Where's Laurence? He'll have to walk you today, I've got too much to do.' Using her wrist, she pushed her hair back and stoked up the fire in the range.

Yesterday, Bea had fallen down the stairs while carrying an armload of sheets and injured her ankle. Bea protested she could still help around the place, but her ankle had swollen so much she couldn't bear any weight on it and Eden insisted she stay in bed for the day. As luck would have it they'd taken in four more lodgers that same morning and now the house was full with five men to take care of as well as themselves. Bea needed more staff, or at least someone to come in and do the washing once a week. Just the cooking and washing alone was bad enough, but to then to all the cleaning, shopping, bed making and everything else was just sapping her energy.

'I won't go.'

She turned back to her daughter, who stood defiant. 'Don't start, I'm warning you.'

Laurence, cheerful as always, breezed into the kitchen holding Lillie's hand. 'We go to school?'

'Yes, Laurence. Take the girls to school and then come straight back. Understand? I need your to help today, so you can't go to the river until later.'

He frowned. 'No river?'

'No, not until later.'

She waved them off from the front step, trying desperately not to be angered by the unkempt state of Josephine. Their battle of wills each day was becoming tiring. She leant against the closed door. Josephine going out in such a state would have horrified Nathan, but she was so exhausted of fighting with her. She blinked away tears. To cry was being indulgent. There was no time to cry, only a household to run.

Josephine waited until they had turned the corner, and Lillie was skipping ahead, before she took Laurence's hand and smiled sweetly up at him. 'Let's go to the river, Laurie.'

He glanced down at her, frowning. 'No... No river today. Eden said.'

'Mam won't mind.' She stopped and tugged his hand. 'We can count the boats.'

'No river today.'

'Let's look at the shops then.' She beamed, knowing he liked peeking through the shop windows at the goods on display.

He scratched his head. 'Must go to school.'

'We'll take Lillie to school and then go to the shops, yes?'

Laurence hesitated, confusion in his eyes. 'Shops?'

'Have you got some pennies?'

He dug around in his trouser pocket and brought out an odd assortment of copper.

'We can buy some sweets.'

'Sweets!' He grinned. 'Treacle toffee?'

'Perhaps.' Josephine nodded, knowing she'd won. They caught up with Lillie and entered the school gates. Once Lillie was surrounded by her friends, Josephine grabbed Laurence's hand again and pulled him away down the road. 'Quick, they can't see me.'

Running and giggling, they were soon lost in the morning crowds of shoppers and city workers. The heady delight of freedom gave Josephine a permanent smile. For hours she and Laurence looked at shop window displays, roamed the streets and ate boiled sweets from a bag Laurence bought.

By midday, they eventually made it down to the river. They walked along the bank out of the city, away from the barges and docks, to the countryside. The sun shone from a clear blue sky and the smell of grass and flowers growing along the banks replaced the stink of town.

Tired, Josephine slumped onto the thick grass sloping down to the water, over her shoulder York basked in the sunshine. 'I'm thirsty.'

'No drink.' Laurence held his hands out wide, before lying down beside her. He rolled onto his back, folding his arms under his head. He grinned, squinting in the sunlight. 'Rest.'

She smiled and copied his pose. The sun warmed her, and the grass was a soft cushion. She yawned and snuggled closer to Laurence.

Josephine woke with a start. Blinking, she sat up, the sun sat low on distant hills and she shivered in the cool evening air. Turning, her heart skipped a beat. Laurence wasn't beside her anymore.

Jumping up, she searched the bank for him. 'Laurie! Laurie!' She scrambled down to the water's edge and looked both ways. Empty. He'd left her! She ran along the top of the bank, following the river back into the city. She darted through the docks, keeping out of the long shadows thrown by the sinking sun. A worker hailed her, but she ducked her head and kept going, holding the stitch in her side.

In her panic she entered the cobbled streets, she skidded to a halt. Nothing looked familiar. Tears welled. She wanted her mam. How would she get home to her mam? She took off again down a long street and turned right at the end. The next street held shops, but none she'd seen before. They weren't the shops her mam or Mrs Prim went to, these had gold painted letterings on their awnings, and assistants standing out the front to open the door for customers.

She ran on, tears blurred her vision and she knocked into a gentleman and fell to her knees.

'Why, I say!' He bent and helped her up, but she jerked away and kept on running. Her knees were bleeding and stung, which made her cry harder. She had to get home.

From the other side of the road, Clifton was climbing out a hired cab. He'd seen the urchin knocked to the ground and something about her face caught his attention. Acting on instinct, he climbed back into the cab and shouted at the driver to follow the girl.

Chapter 16

Eden paced the kitchen, her arms wrapped around her waist. Again, she glanced out the small window to the growing darkness outside. Where was Josephine?

Laurence shifted in his chair, his shoulders bowed since Eden had raged at him for leaving Josephine alone, and not remembering where.

Bea, who had hobbled down the stairs because of Eden's shouting, sat at the table. She'd heard the tale and when the men came in from work had asked them to immediately go out again and look for Josephine, which Eden was thankful for. Bea poured out more tea. 'Likely the little scamp is doing this on purpose.'

Gritting her teeth, Eden stared at her. 'She wouldn't stay out this late.'

'She's defiant.'

'She was with Laurence. He shouldn't have left her.' Eden glared at the young man, suddenly hating him for his disability. 'Go out there and look for her! Go to every place you visited today. Go!'

Alarmed, he looked from Eden to his mother. 'Ma?'

'Calm down, Eden, really. You're overacting. All the lodgers are looking for her. They'll be going along the river and searching the streets. Laurence isn't going out there now. He'll do no good...' Bea pushed the teacup across the table to her. 'I bet the men will come walking through the door with her any minute.'

'And what if they don't? What if something has happened to her? What if she fell in the river?' she snapped, as horrifying images clouded her mind. 'What if it was Laurence out there?'

'Well, she should have gone to school as she was told to do. That girl is too forthright as it is. She needs to be controlled. I don't understand why you let her get away with half the stuff she does.'

'Don't tell me how to raise my child.' Anger built to vie for supremacy over her worry.

'I won't have you placing the blame on Laurence because of her waywardness. I'm telling you, she'll be doing this on purpose to scare you. She wants to go back to her home, that's what this is all about.'

'We can't go back.'

'Why?' Bea's expression turned suspicious. 'I've kept my counsel all these weeks, but if you're in trouble I want to know. Are you on the run from the law?'

'No!'

'Well something's not right, I can feel it. I don't want trouble brought to my doorstep and if you are hiding something from me, then you can pack your things and go.'

Eden felt the blood drain from her face. 'I've done nothing but work hard for you.'

'Aye, and I've put a roof over your head and food in your belly.'

'I worked for it while you were sick in bed,' she shouted. 'Everything we received I worked for. You wouldn't have lodgers now if it wasn't for me. While you were sick did you expect Laurence to run the house? Have sense woman!' Not wanting to say anything else she may later regret, Eden went to the back door and yanked it open. Despite having all the lodgers out roaming the streets for Josephine, she couldn't stay in the house and do nothing.

'Mam?' Lillie, her eyes wide and frightened, slid her hand into Eden's. 'Can I come too?'

'No, pet. Stay with Mrs Prim.' Eden kissed her cheek and looked at Bea, hoping she would do this favour for her. 'I have to go search.'

Bea nodded, sympathy and apology in her eyes. She held out her hand for Lillie. 'Come here, little one, and I'll read you a story.'

Throwing a shawl around her shoulders, Eden then left the house, hurried down to the dark cut and dashed along it to the street. A man, one of the neighbours, strolled by whistling, and she asked him if he'd seen Josephine. He hadn't. A young woman was walking home, carrying a basket of goods. Eden asked her the same question and received the same response.

Eden lifted her skirts and ran down the street, looking into all the cuts and alleys as she passed, calling Josephine's name. Several times she ran to knock on neighbours' doors and asked them if they'd seen her. They hadn't, and they'd told the lodgers the same thing.

She stood in the middle of the dim street and felt utterly alone. She couldn't lose her daughter. Hadn't she suffered enough?

Gripping her skirts, she ran down the street. If she went to the police, they could help search for her too. She rounded the corner and banged straight into a child, who screamed. They both fell to the road with a thump.

'Josephine!' Eden scrambled on her knees over to her and gathered her into her arms. 'Where have you been?'

'Mam.' Josephine sobbed into her chest.

They sat on the road in a tangle of skirts, rocking and crying.

Eden took Josephine's face in her hands. 'Don't you ever do this again, do you hear me? Not ever!'

'I'm sorry. I got lost.' Tears had streaked her dirty face.

'I've been so worried.' Eden wiped away her own tears of relief.

'Laurence left me at the river.'

'You know what he's like. He can't be trusted to do anything properly, but the blame isn't his entirely. You did wrong by not going to school. I should whip your backside red and blue, my girl.'

'Can we go home to grandfather? Please, mam, *please*. I'll behave forever if we go home.'

'We can't, not yet, but I've written again to Grandfather asking him to come here.' Eden stood and helped Josephine up.

'It's not the same. I miss home.'

'I know, darling, I know.' Eden glanced at a cab pulling into the end of the street as she tucked Josephine closer to her, wanting to reassure herself that her daughter was safe.

'I'm hungry.' Josephine sniffed.

'Your dinner is in the oven keeping warm.' Eden kissed the top of her head, then took a deep breath to slow her frantic heartbeat. Arm in arm they walked back to the lodging house.

~ ~ ~

Early the following morning, Eden dusted the furniture in the front room, listening to Lillie chatting with Bea in the kitchen. She stacked the newspaper neatly on the small table by a chair and moved on. Josephine was upstairs sleeping off the effects of yesterday's drama, Laurence was out the back burning rubbish and the men gone to their work in various parts of York.

Pausing in wiping the mantelpiece, she thought about the evening before, shivering at the terror she felt. Josephine had played out her worst fears without realising it. That's how she'd have felt had Clifton taken her. But it hadn't been him, Josephine had done it all on her own.

She sat on a chair by the fireplace, tormented. Well into the night she had spoken to both girls about behaving, of not going off alone ever, but was it enough? How could she watch them every minute of every day? Back at the cottage, she'd always had Nathan and grandfather to help raise them, now the worry was hers alone. Perhaps she should return home? Was the risk of something happening to the girls greater than in this great city? Clifton wouldn't find them here, but there were other dangers. A child could be lost in the streets and never seen again.

A knock on the door interrupted her thoughts. At this early hour, she wondered who'd be knocking on the front door. 'I'll get it, Bea.'

'Right you are.' She called from the kitchen.

Eden sighed and left the room. She'd have to talk with Bea today and straighten things out. Last night had been too fraught with emotions for a serious discussion. She turned the handle and opened the door and jumped back in surprise as it was thrust against her, banging her into wall. Clifton's grin blocked out everything else.

'Eden, my lovely, I've missed you.'

She screamed, but he whacked the side of her head with his cane. Pain exploded across her ear. He slammed the door shut and turned to face Bea and Lillie who raced into the hallway.

'Who are you?' Bea demanded, pushing Lillie behind her.

Clifton advanced on her, but she held her ground until he was mere inches from her, then a blow from his fist into her stomach crumbled her to the ground. Lillie cried out, her eyes wide in shock.

Eden lunged and landed on his back. She was aware of Lillie crying, but focused on getting the monster out of the house. She hit him about the head. Clifton cursed and tossed her off him. As she landed on the floor, he booted in the ribs.

'Mam,' Lillie screamed, and it echoed around the house.

Eden reached for her, doubled up with pain, but Clifton grabbed Eden and dragged her into the front room and slammed her into a chair. She went to get up, but a powerful backhand sent her sprawling, she landed with a gasp on the carpet. Dazed, she couldn't focus. She tasted blood in her mouth. Her arms and legs refused to move. Lillie's screaming was abruptly cut off and Eden felt her heart stop. On hands and knees, she crawled across the floor towards the door. Noise and confusion came from the hallway. She heard Laurence's voice, then a bang and a thud. Once at the door, she used it to help heave herself to her feet.

'Mam!' Josephine raced down the stairs and clutched her side. They stared at Clifton who, huffing and puffing, was dragging a limp Laurence towards them.

'Clifton what are you doing?' Panic and horror filled her.

He ignored her and continued into the front room, where he dumped Laurence on the floor. He glowered at Eden and pointed to the sofa by the window. 'Sit over there and don't move or I'll kill you all.'

Without Lillie, she couldn't make a run for it. She nodded and, wracked with pain, gingerly walked to the sofa with Josephine clinging to her skirts. 'Where's Lillie?'

Clifton paused at the door and smiled. 'Safe. For now.'

'And Bea?'

'The same. Is there anyone else in the house?'

'No.'

He slid the bolt home on the front door and then disappeared down the hallway again.

'That's Uncle Charlie's cousin, Mam.' Josephine shook and Eden held her close.

'Yes, love. Be quiet now.' They waited in silence and Clifton returned a moment later. She watched him peer out the window and satisfied all was quiet, he turned back to her.

'So, Eden.' He glanced around the room. 'This is where you bolted to.'

'What do you want?'

'Silly question.'

'You can't have her.'

He stepped closer to Laurence, ignoring her, and peered down at the boy. He snorted and toed Laurence with his shoe but got no response.

'You've knocked him out cold,' she snapped. 'Leave him alone. You've done enough.'

Clifton straightened, but his expression wasn't one of gloating anymore, but instead resembled panic. He edged away from the boy. 'Come on. We're leaving.'

'I don't think so.' Eden glared up at him. She held onto Josephine tightly. 'No more, Clifton. You've ruined my life for too long and I'm sick of it.' She stood and took a step closer to him, no longer frightened. 'We'll never be with you.'

Anger tightened his features and he whipped out a pistol to wave it in her face. 'Better off dead do you think then?'

Her stomach curled into a knot, but she stared at him and raised her eyebrows. 'Yes, likely we would be.'

'You bitch!' His piggish eyes narrowed, and he pointed the pistol straight at her face. 'I will kill you for what you've done to me.'

'What I've done to you? That's a laugh, isn't it?'

Clifton glanced at Laurence and the weapon wavered. '*You* made me kill him.'

Eden frowned. 'What?' She looked down at Laurence, and at this angle she could see his half-opened eyes. She stifled a cry and fell to her knees beside him. 'Laurence! Laurence, wake up.' She felt for his heartbeat and his pulse, but she was shaking too much to feel anything. 'He-he might be just unconscious. Send for a doctor, Clifton, quickly.'

'I didn't hit him that hard.' Clifton backed away, the pistol quivering in his hand. 'He's dead. But I only wanted to knock him out, not kill him.' He stared at Eden, his face turning a sickly white shade. 'Truly, I never meant…'

Eden rocked back, a hand to her mouth. She was going to be sick.

'Mam?' Josephine ran to huddle beside her.

Slowly, Eden raised her gaze to Clifton. 'Your actions have killed another.'

'I didn't mean it.' He glanced around widely. 'Hurry up, we have to go.'

'You can't run from this one, Clifton.'

'Shut up!' He grabbed her arm and hauled her up. 'You, girl, come with us,' he demanded to Josephine.

Yanking her arm out of his grasp, Eden's anger took over. 'I said no!' She hit him about the head, fisting and kicking him. He backed away only to fall over a chair and tumble to the ground.

Eden snatched the pistol from his hand and calmly levelled it at his head. She cocked her head to one side. 'Who is the hunted now?'

'Let me go.' He cringed, one hand raised in surrender. 'I promise to leave you alone.'

~ ~ ~

Joel thanked the woman for her time and stepped away from her door. Another house, another door. Across the street, Charlie stood talking to another woman on her doorstep. How many streets, houses, doors and people had they visited and nothing. Not one person had seen them. Annabella and Carleton were in the next street doing the same as him, knocking on doors, asking strangers if they'd seen a woman with two little girls.

He straightened his shoulders and mentally chastised himself. This was only the beginning of second day, he couldn't expect miracles right away. They'd only covered the area closest to the train station; there were many more streets to go yet. Grey clouds covered the sky and a stiff breeze was picking up, the weather didn't appear to be very summery today.

He went up the next set of steps and knocked on the polished door. After a couple of minutes of waiting, an elderly man opened it. 'Aye?'

'Good morning. Sorry to disturb you but I'm wondering if you could help me.' Joel smiled. 'I'm looking for a woman by the name of Eden Harris. She has two small girls. I was told they may have come to live in this area.'

The old man scratched his white stubbly chin. 'Harris...Harris. Can't say I know the name...'

Inwardly, Joel groaned, but continued to smile as he thanked the man.

'Wait a minute...' the fellow frowned, 'now I think of it, Mrs Prim took in a woman with two girls a couple of months back.'

Joel's heart somersaulted. 'Mrs Prim?'

'Aye, she owns the lodging house at the end of the street, last house. I often see the young ones playing in the street.' He leant against the door jamb. 'Actually, only last night...no...no, it wasn't last night as I was the pub last night and wasn't home. It must have been the night before that, for I was home that night. My missus was cooking kippers for supper. Yes, that's right. We were talking about the price of kippers. It's gone up, you know, the price from the market, by a tuppence a pound.'

Joel leaned forward, silently begging the old man to hurry up and get to the point before he shook it out of him. 'And the girls?'

'Ah, yes. There was a hullabaloo about one of the little lasses going missing. One of their lodgers came knocking asking if we'd seen her. Then later the mother came.' He turned back to the hall. 'Oye, Edith! Did they find that young lass from Prim's?'

An equally old woman shuffled up the hall from the kitchen beyond. 'Aye, they did. I heard it from Rita at the grocer's shop on the corner yesterday. Safe and well she is.' She smiled at Joel. 'Children do that, you know, run off or come home late. Don't know what they do to their parents they don't.'

Her husband nodded beside her. 'We had three boys. My, they were trouble at times, but they've grown into good men with families of their own now.'

'Aye, families of their own now,' the wife echoed.

Joel edged down one step, eager to be on his way to find this Prim's house. 'Thank you very much for your time.'

'Did you want to come in for a cup of tea?' The man stepped forward. 'Edith put the kettle on.'

'No, no.' Joel backed down another step. 'Thank you, very much, but no, I must be on my way.' He nodded, smiled and thanked them again. The old man looked ready to speak once more, and Joel waved effectively halting him before jumping the last step and hurrying up the street to Charlie, who was rushing to meet him.

In the middle of the street they spoke as one. 'Prim's Lodging House.'

Charlie sucked in a breath. 'It's the last house.'

They both turned and stared at it.

Suddenly, Joel couldn't move. For so long he'd been waiting to see her, and now he couldn't take the last steps to achieve that dream. His throat went dry, blood pounded in his ears. Inside that house was Eden. The woman he loved.

'Are we going to knock on the door or stand here all morning staring at it?' Charlie grinned.

'I haven't been this frightened since…Lord, I don't think I have ever been this frightened.'

'Not even facing wild Boers?'

'Not even then. I was trained for them, but not for this.'

'She needs us,' Charlie murmured.

Those three words were what he required. He jerked forward, striding towards the house, to Eden, to the future.

~ ~ ~

'Mam?'

Eden didn't take her gaze off Clifton. 'Go to the kitchen and look for Lillie.'

Josephine slid past Clifton just as knocking came at the door. They all froze.

'Don't answer it,' Clifton whispered, sweat beading his forehead.

'Answer it.' She nodded to Josephine, who raced out of the room.

Clifton scrambled to his feet. 'I beg you, Eden. *Please.*'

From the hall they heard Josephine squeal happily. Eden frowned. No one made her do that unless she loved them. *Grandfather?* She inched forward trying to see who was there. She didn't want her grandfather coming into this mess, but on the other hand she desperately needed him with her.

'Eden,' Clifton stepped towards the door, 'let me go. I'll slip out the back and no one will know I've been. You can say the boy fell and banged his head. I—'

'I don't think so, Clifton.' Joel stood in the doorway.

Joel? Eden's knees trembled at the sight of him. She badly needed to sit down or cry or both. She

200

blinked, wondering if she was seeing things. Was that really him? The pistol wavered in her hand, it was heavy and her hand ached, but she couldn't lose focus. As much as she wanted to look at Joel properly, she had to concentrate on Clifton.

'W-When did you arrive?' Clifton goggled at Joel. Sweat ran down his cheeks.

Joel turned to Charlie who'd come to stand behind him. 'Send for the police, Charlie.'

'No!' Clifton fell to his knees and begged. 'Not the police. I didn't mean it. It was an accident.'

'Your time of harassment is over, cousin,' Joel spat. 'Take it like a man for once.'

'I won't, I tell you.' Clifton jerked to his feet. 'I'll not go to prison for this.' He spun and leapt for Eden. She screamed and fired. Clifton's howl of pain filled the house. He dropped at her feet.

The pistol fell from her hand. The smell of gunpowder stung her nose. Clifton was moaning, writhing on the carpet, clutching his leg where blood seeped through his trousers.

She slowly sank to the floor and gave in to the blackness claiming her.

Chapter 17

She had periods of being awake, of hearing noises, whispers, the touch of a hand, the coolness of water on her lips and then peaceful silence. She liked the quiet. Had there ever been a time when she had complete quietness in her life? She doubted it.

Light on her eyes drew her from the haziness in her mind to the present. Beside her came the rustle of a dress. Eden turned her head, opened her eyes and squinted against the lamplight.

'Mam?'

'Jo…' her voice came out as a croak.

'Yes, it's me.' Josephine's face came closer, blocking out some of the light. 'They told me not to wake you.'

'But you did.' She smiled at her wayward daughter.

'I was frightened.'

'Why?'

'I thought you might not wake up.' Her bottom lip trembled, and tears glistened in her eyes.

'Oh darling.' Eden reached up and cupped her cheek. 'I'll never leave you, I promise.'

'Can I sleep with you?'

Eden moved over, her body aching in protest. Someone had dressed her in her white nightgown. 'What time is it?'

'Nearly morning.' Josephine climbed in and snuggled close.

'Really?' Amazed Eden focused on the curtains and the greyish light seeping around the edges. She turned down the lamp. 'Where's Lillie?'

'Sleeping with Mrs Prim.'

It all came flooding back to her. A day from Hell. She swallowed and stroked Josephine's hair. 'What-what happened to Clifton?'

'Uncle Charlie and his brother,' she yawned, 'they sent for the police. He was taken away and so was Laurence. Mrs Prim has cried all afternoon and night. Lillie stayed with her.'

'Is Lillie all right?'

She yawned again. 'Yer, she fell asleep early and Mrs Prim said she could sleep with her. But Aunty Bella wasn't happy as she wanted us to go to a hotel with her.'

'Aunty Bella is here too,' Eden mused, her thoughts shying away from Joel. She was too tired, too utterly exhausted to think of anything anymore. Her girls were safe, that's all that mattered. She cuddled Josephine closer and closed her eyes. She'd deal with it all in the morning.

It seemed she'd only been asleep for mere minutes when she heard voices. Josephine stirred beside her and stretched.

'Well, it's about time, I must say.' Annabella's impatient tone made Eden smile before she'd even opened her eyes. She blinked and held out her hand. It was grasped tightly, and Annabella kissed her forehead. 'Dearest.'

Sitting up, Eden untangled herself from Josephine, who lay sleepily watching them. Annabella looked radiant in a dress of shimmering blue-grey silk. Her golden hair swept up in an array of curls and white ribbons. Eden felt like an old woman and was sure she resembled one too. She smiled at her dear friend. 'How are you, Bella?'

'Lord,' Annabella waved her hand dismissively, 'I'm perfectly fine, or I will be once you and the girls are home at Bradbury.'

Eden thought of the Hall, the estate, the woodland and her grandfather. 'I'll be glad to be home too.'

'Josephine, poppet, do get up and find Lillie. It's time for you to be dressed.' Annabella went around the bed to Josephine's side and helped her out. 'There's breakfast in the kitchen, I brought it with me for you.'

Once Josephine had dawdled from the room, Annabella sat on the wooden chair beside the bed and grasped Eden's hand again. 'Now...'

Studying her friend, seeing the torment in her eyes, Eden braced herself for the words to come. 'Tell me everything.'

Annabella nodded. 'Clifton has been charged with murdering that poor young man, Mrs Prim's son.'

'Poor Bea. He was all she had.' Eden sighed, for of the times Laurence tested her patience with his slowness, she had still grown fond of him.

'Mrs Prim will testify against Clifton, as she saw him hit her son.'

'I will testify too, for Clifton admitted it to me.'

'Good. The case against him will be stronger.' Annabella gazed down at their joined hands. 'There is other news. Terribly sad news.'

'Grandfather.' Eden swallowed passed the knot of emotion in her throat. She didn't need Annabella to confirm what she most feared. Grandfather would have come by now if he'd been able. Her last letter, posted two days ago on the morning Josephine played truant from school, had been insistent that she needed him. He'd not have ignored that unless something had prevented him.

'I'm so sorry.'

'What happened?'

'Clifton. He—'

'No.' Eden climbed stiffly out of bed. 'Don't tell me. Not yet. I don't want to hear it. Perhaps later…'

'I've ordered the carriage.' Annabella sniffed away threatening tears. 'We are leaving soon. I've come to help you and the girls to get ready. Joel and Charlie are with the police, sorting all that out.'

Eden wrapped her dressing gown around her. 'I must see Bea.'

'Of course.' Annabella stood. 'I'll go find the girls and help them.'

They parted on the landing, Annabella went downstairs while Eden crossed to the bedroom opposite and slightly tapped on the door and entered. Bea sat on the end of the bed. Dressed in black, her back was stiff, her features composed. She didn't look at her and simply stared at the wall.

'Bea?' Eden stepped closer to the bed. Cold and bare, with only the basic furniture, the bedroom's stark atmosphere contributed to its owner's controlled personality. 'Bea, I'm so sorry.'

'So, you should be.'

Bea's quiet words halted Eden's next step. 'I never believed Clifton would find me here.'

'But he did.'

'If I'd known he would find us and put you and Laurence in danger, I would have moved on.'

'But you didn't.'

Eden's stomach twisted. 'Nothing I can say-'

Jerking to her feet, Bea turned eyes full of hate on Eden. 'Leave my house. Take your trouble and go. There is money on the table for your wages. I never want to see you again.'

'I am going, but I don't want your money and I don't want to leave on bad terms.'

Bea's fists showed white around the knuckles. 'Bad terms? My son is dead. I don't give a fig for what you want.'

'You aren't the only one suffering. I've lost loved ones, too. I understand your grief. Clifton killed my husband and my grandfather, and he stole my innocence. So, I know your pain.'

Bea turned away; her expression unchanged. 'Go away. Go with you wealthy friends and leave me to bury my son.'

'I can stay, if you need-'

'No, I don't want you here.'

Eden glanced down at her hands, seeking the right words. 'For what it's worth, I admire you and I'm deeply sorry for what's happened. If you ever need help, please send a note to Bradbury Hall, near Gargrave.'

'I never will. I repeat, I never want to see you again.'

'I'm sorry.' Filled with guilt and sadness, Eden returned to her own room and dressed quickly. After packing her and the girls' belongings, she carried their luggage downstairs. She could do no more to help Bea.

'Mam.' Lillie rushed up the hallway with Josephine and Annabella following.

'Good morning, my sweet.' Eden bent and kissed Lillie's cheek. She looked at Annabella. 'Are we ready?'

'Yes, the carriage is waiting.'

Eden took a deep breath and led them outside. A few neighbours stood in the street; their whispers ceased as they saw Eden emerge. She climbed into the Bradbury carriage, her emotions lurching between sorrow and regret and anxiety about going home. The girls sat on either side of her while Annabella gave instructions for the luggage to be loaded, then they were trundling away down the street and out of York – leaving one kind of devastation behind and journeying towards another. *Oh Grandfather...*

~ ~ ~

Eden stood alone beside the grave, staring down at the polished coffin. Birds sang in the trees edging the churchyard. The first day of July and it was too beautiful for a funeral. Brilliant sunshine bathed the countryside, flowers bloomed, fat lambs frolicked beside their mothers in lush grass. Grandfather would have enjoyed such a day. He'd have sat out on his chair in a sun patch, watching the girls play.

She allowed a single tear to escape, her first sign of the pressuring ache inside. She shouldn't cry, for if she started, she doubted she would stop. Nathan and now grandfather. How would she cope without them?

The villagers had dwindled away, gone to drink Earnshaw's ale in remembrance of Horatio Morley. They asked her to go back with them, but she declined. She hadn't wanted to chat with old friends or return to the Hall with the others. Instead, she just wanted to stay out in the sunlight, close to the grave, to Grandfather and all the other relatives buried here. Lifting her gaze, she read her parent's inscription on their headstone only yards away, and then her grandmother's. She smiled lovingly at Nathan's grave behind Grandfather's.

So many people she had loved and lost. Footsteps sounded behind her and she braced herself in case it was Joel.

For the last three days while she and the girls had been living at the Hall, she kept to the rooms Annabella gave them. The girls shared one bedroom and Eden had another larger room with its own small sitting-room. There, she had listened to Charlie tell of Grandfather's last moments. In prison, Clifton had confessed to beating her grandfather and setting the cottage alight. Grief kept her from going downstairs and Joel never once knocked on her door. She was surprised by the hurt that caused.

Why hadn't he knocked?

Why couldn't she face him?

'Eden.'

She held her breath. It was him. Joel came to stand beside her, his gaze locked on the coffin below. They stood for several minutes in silence and Eden felt the pressure inside her build.

She didn't look at him, yet his presence overwhelmed her; the stiffness of his uniform, the solidness of his size. Not since the morning he entered Bea's house had she looked at him, and even then, it had been only a glance. She couldn't fight the urge now.

Slowly, with painful awareness, she turned her head to look at him and seeing his handsome profile so close sent her to her knees.

'Eden!' Joel knelt beside her, holding her upright. 'What is it? Let me take you home.'

Tears blurred her vision. She held up a gloved hand and touched his cheek. Was he really here, after all this time? His blue eyes softened as she traced the lines running nose to mouth. Grey peppered the dark hair at his temples beneath his uniform cap. Creases fanned the corner of his eyes and the African sun had tanned his skin. The young, dashing hero she had loved so long ago was now a mature man. He'd changed as much as she, and her tears flowed because of it. A sob broke from her at the wasted years, the shattered hopes and dreams she once held so dear. Though they had never spoken of their love, he had been hers and she his.

'I've missed you,' she whispered.

Joel cupped her cheek in his hand. He softly spoke her name with such a tender look that it was the last straw. 'My beautiful Eden.'

She couldn't bear the pain anymore. Jolting to her feet, she stumbled on the uneven ground. He reached out, but she ignored the help and ran from him. Joel called out her name, but she kept running, not stopping until she was in the middle of the village. She ducked down a lane between two shops and into the back of Earnshaw's pub. Crates and barrels littered the cobbled yard. A mangy cat jumped on top of the fence. Eden staggered over to lean against an outbuilding wall and cried brokenly for all she had lost.

'Lass?'

She spun and stared at Eddie Earnshaw. Embarrassed, she wiped at her cheeks. 'I-I'm sorry.'

'Nay lass, what you got to be sorry for?' His kind round face brought fresh tears to her eyes. 'Will you not come inside for a drink? Everyone's in there and to be honest I'm tired of looking at their faces. I'd much rather see your pretty face on the other side of the bar.'

'I couldn't.'

'Why?' He frowned and then smiled. 'Horatio is going to be sadly missed and everyone wants to talk about him. What would be a better way to spend the afternoon than to be with people who can tell you stories from years ago? Horatio always loved a good wake. A drink, a natter and food. Tell me there's nowt better.'

The tension eased from her shoulders and she looked beyond him to the pub. Suddenly the idea of being surrounded by her grandfather's friends felt right. They were her people too, and Nathan's. She'd seen his father at the funeral today and one of his cousins. Yes, she very much wanted to be with those people who knew and loved the ones she'd lost. For one afternoon she'd forget about being a mother, a friend of the Bradbury's, her tortured past and just relax in the presence of those who expected nothing from her.

Chapter 18

'What do you mean?' Annabella stared at her and then at Charlie. 'Speak to her, Charlie!'

Charlie rubbed his forehead. 'I don't often agree with my sister, but in this I do. You can't leave again, Eden.'

Eden rolled her eyes and walked to the drawing-room window, watching out for the returning carriage. The minute Joel entered the house she would go back upstairs. The connection they shared alarmed her. Two days ago, at the graveside, he had given her a glimpse of the past when he had loved her.

What did he feel now? How would it alter her life this time? Did he intend to act on his feelings or ignore them? She didn't know this older Joel. Yet, their bond still existed. Her body and heart knew him.

She sighed, despondency welling. It was all too complicated - too damn hard. He would have to marry soon, to carry on the Bradbury line. Her heart shrivelled at the prospect. She wouldn't remain here to witness that. 'I can't stay.'

'You'll be the death of me.' Annabella flounced over to the chair and plopped herself on to it. 'Why are you being so selfish? The girls won't want to leave again. We don't want you to go, so why do it?'

She closed her eyes and tried to think of a good excuse. She wanted to scream at them that she couldn't live in the same house as Joel, that her heart could take no more. Finally, she turned back to them.' There are too many memories here.'

Charlie folded his arms. 'I understand that, but is the answer to be somewhere alone again? Yes, there are good and bad memories here, but there are also people who care for you.'

'I know...' She was torn as always when it came to this family.

'You need a holiday.' Annabella bounced up, her eyes bright.

'You need time away from here, from all that's happened. A holiday is a much better solution.'

'I can't afford a holiday. I have no money, nothing.' The thought chilled her. She was dependant on the Bradburys' goodwill at the moment. With the cottage burnt to the ground, she had no home of her own and no income.

Charlie frowned. 'I've been thinking about that and talking it over with Joel-'

'No, I don't want to be the housekeeper again, Charlie, thanks all the same.'

He shook his head. 'I wasn't going to suggest that. We, Joel and I were thinking that we could offer to buy the land the cottage stood on. What do you think? It would give you some capital to start again.'

Eden stared, her mind whirling. 'The land?'

'Yes. Unless you had ideas of rebuilding another cottage and living there?'

At night, when unable to sleep, she had tossed around the idea of rebuilding and living there with the girls. She could, perhaps, obtain work in the village. 'I did have some thought of doing that, but nothing confirmed in my mind.'

'Well, it was just a suggestion.'

Annabella clapped her hands. 'I know! One of Carleton's new friends has this little cottage by the sea near Whitby. He said we could use it any time we wanted. You could go there for a while and rest. What do you think?'

'You are allowed to use it, not me.' Eden gave her a wry smile.

'Nonsense. When I explain you're like a sister to me then they'll agree.'

'I don't know, Bella.'

Charlie stood and kissed Bella's cheek. 'It's perfect. Well done.'

'I'll go to Carleton immediately and make some inquiries.' Annabella beamed and called for Mellors, who'd become the butler, valet and general mainstay of the house in Eden's absence.

Charlie laughed. 'I'm sure we can wait until your husband returns here this evening, Bella.'

Annabella paused. 'Well, yes, I suppose so.' She grimaced. 'And it will save me from seeing my mother-in-1aw.'

Eden tapped her fingers together. A cottage by the sea. The idea took hold and warmed her. 'How long could we stay?'

'As long as you like. Carleton's friend, Mr Hobson, lives in London most of the time and the cottage is only used in the middle of summer for a few weeks as far as I know.'

'I would like to visit the sea. The girls would be so excited.'

'Then it's done.' Annabella grinned. 'If the cottage is vacant, we'll go right away.'

Charlie looked at his sister. 'We? I thought this was for Eden and the girls only?'

Annabella pouted. 'They don't want to be alone, Charlie.'

Eden went to protest the statement, but Annabella continued, 'The sea air would do wonders for you and time together for Carleton and me is exactly what we need.'

'How big is this cottage?' Charlie sighed.

'Oh, I heard it had seven bedrooms. Plenty of room for us all.'

'I doubt Joel will want to go. He's only just returned home. He has things to do here and plans of his own.'

'Then Joel will miss out. Besides, he should want to have a small holiday with his family. It's been years since we were all together.'

'Well, ask him and see what he says.' Eden turned away from them. The last thing her confused feelings needed was Joel to be included. She looked out of the window at the flowerbeds blooming in the sunshine. 'I'm going for a walk,' she announced and before they had a chance to say they'd accompany her, she swept from the room and met Mellors in the hall.

He whipped out his handkerchief and patted the sweat beaded forehead. 'I was just coming. Did you need anything? I was outside with the girls.'

'The girls?'

'Yes,' he smiled, 'they are intent on paddling in the lake, but I said we'd have to ask you first.'

She placed her hand on his arm. 'Thank you for spending time with them. They adore you so.'

'Nay, it's my pleasure. They are the children I never had, and their presence here lightens everyone's heart.'

She kissed his cheek in thanks, not just for today but all the days he'd been such a support to her and this family. 'You rest. I'll take the girls to the lake.'

'It's hot out there. Cook has a basket of food waiting, so don't forget it.' His hand covered hers briefly before he marched into the drawing-room to tend to Annabella and Charlie.

After collecting the basket and her black straw hat, Eden left the house in search of the girls. She found them by the pond, their bonnets pushed back and their faces inches from the surface, giggling and laughing. Eden smiled the sight lifting some of the sadness from her. She would always have her girls and they would grow up having each other.

Eden held the basket high. 'Fancy a picnic by the lake?'

Josephine and Lillie scrambled up and whooped. They ran off towards the lake and Eden followed, sauntering along through the gardens, smelling the flowers on the air. She paused on the slope that went down to the water's edge watching the girls.

'You can take off your boots and stockings if you want, but don't go in too far.' She placed the basket on the lush grass at her feet as the girls splashed their hands and squealed.

Sitting on the grass, she spread out her black skirt, opened the basket and poked about. Cook had packed chicken, bread, apples, strawberries, shortbread, slices of currant cakes and a bottle of lemon water.

'May I join you?'

Eden squinted up. Joel towered over her, a smile hovering. 'Er…yes, of course.'

'I can go if you prefer?'

'N-no.' She squirmed inwardly at her unconvincing tone. She looked away and stared at the girls. His presence set her trembling.

Joel sat down and rubbed his injured shoulder. They remained quiet for several minutes, then he shifted his position.

'I don't want to spoil your day, but you need to know the latest news.'

Eden stiffened. 'Oh?'

He pulled at the grass and then glanced up at her. 'I've been to York.'

'To see a doctor, wasn't it?'

'Yes, but that was not all. This morning, before I left, I received a message.' He frowned and rubbed his forehead. 'Clifton managed to hang himself last night.'

Bowing her head, Eden closed her eyes in relief. It was over.

Never again would she have to look at his face or even think about him. Dead and gone. She nodded at Joel in thanks. 'He caused so much pain and anguish. I know he's your cousin but I'm not sorry he's done it.'

'He was no longer family, and his demise can only bring relief to many people. Even my Aunt Ada will be spared the humiliation of a trial and her son being in prison.'

'Yes.'

He took her hand and rubbed his thumb across her knuckles.

'Try not to think of him. You are free of him.'

The girls came bounding up the bank only to stop uncertainly on seeing Joel sitting there.

Eden removed her hand from his. 'We have a guest for our picnic. Isn't that lovely?'

He smiled such a devastatingly handsome smile that both girls took a step closer to him. He opened up the basket. 'Are you hungry?'

They glanced from Joel to Eden and back again.

'Cook used to make great hampers for us when we were children, didn't she, Eden?'

Eden nodded slowly, her heart thumping as she remembered how close they once were. She'd forgotten more times they were together than she recalled, and her mind brimmed with memories.

'Did you know my mam when she was little?' Josephine stared at him.

'Of course, he did.' She quickly took food out of the basket. 'You know the stories of us all growing up together. Aunty Bella has told you numerous tales.'

Josephine knelt on the grass and studied Joel. 'Yes, but. . .'

Joel laughed. 'She doesn't know me, Eden. She can place Charlie and Bella with you, but not me, someone she's only recently met.'

Eden kept busy spreading out the food as Joel gave his attention to the girls. He told them tales of Africa, the animals and birds, the people, the food and scenery. Soon, Eden lost her nervousness and listened to him with the same rapt interest as the girls. She wanted to learn about him, to understand the man he had become.

After the girls had eaten and run out of questions, they scampered off to the water again and Eden packed up the basket.

'You have two beautiful daughters, Eden.'

She glanced up and smiled. 'Thank you.'

'Josephine is very much like you were as a child. She's a clever one.'

'Cheeky more like, and independent.'

'Like you used to be.'

'Was I? I don't remember.'

'I do. I recall everything. All the times we laughed and the scrapes we got into. How happy a time it was then.'

'And so long ago.' She wrapped the bread in a linen cloth.

He twirled a grass stem between his thumb and fingers. 'Is Lillie like her father?'

She hesitated only slightly at his mention of Nathan. 'Yes, in nature she is. He was quiet and good, like Lillie.'

'I'm pleased he made you a fine husband.'

'He saved me from being alone with a baby. Not many men would do that. His love...his love helped me survive one of the worst times of my life.'

'If I'd stayed-'

'Don't Joel.' She thrust the bread into the basket, her stomach twisting. 'What is done cannot be changed. We cannot live with regrets.'

Joel gazed out over the lake. 'I hear you're going away for a while. To some cottage near the coast?'

'Yes, at Annabella's suggestion.'

'I too am going away.'

Her heart banged against her chest and she focused on fastening the toggle on the basket. 'Oh?'

'To London. To see if my shoulder can be fixed.'

'Then I wish you well.'

'I hope I can come visit you at the cottage once I return?'

'Of course. We will all be there.'

'Eden.' She raised her eyes to him and saw the longing reflected in his. 'I know you've had your share of pain and suffering. ..'

'We all have that in our lives, Joel.' She stood, stalling his next words and called to the girls. They'd shared a wonderful couple of hours, and she didn't want the conversation moving to more difficult subjects. She wasn't ready to examine her feelings or her needs just yet. Joel stood also and took his cap off to rake his hand through his dark hair. 'I've been wanting to talk to you.'

'Oh?'

'I have plans of travelling. I'd like to go back to Africa at some point.'

'I see.' She found it hard to swallow. He was leaving again.

'Not just Africa, of course, but other places, India and the East, and Southern Europe as well. I think the warmer climates would suit Charlie, too. I haven't asked him yet, but I want him to agree. What do you think?'

'Yes, indeed. The winters here are terrible for him.'

'I was hoping you and the girls would like to travel with us.''

She stared in surprise. 'You want us to go with you?'

'Absolutely.' He stepped closer, his gaze not wavering from her face. 'I couldn't face leaving you again. The last time I did it nearly killed me, and I dare not risk it a second time.'

She saw the love in his eyes and her body tingled in awareness.

'Wh-when do you plan to leave?'

'I was thinking of waiting a year or two, but for Charlie's sake, I think it would benefit him to leave before the cold weather arrives. So possibly within a few months.'

'I thought you had plans for the estate?'

'They can wait, Charlie's health cannot. If I'm only to have a few years left with him, I want them to be good years. The estate will survive, and I can return to it later, when I'm too old to travel.' He grinned and she itched to touch him, to run her fingers through his hair. 'So, will you come with us? There are so many places I want to share with you, Eden.'

'May I think about it? I have to consider the girls.'

'Certainly.' His expression became serious once more. 'I know it might be too soon for you to think of this, but should you wish to one day remarry, I hope…I hope you will think of me first. But even if you do not wish to marry me, I'd still be happy for you to come with us.'

Her mouth gaped in shock, but the girls joined them before she could respond. Together, they walked back towards the Hall with the girls talking to Joel as easily as if they'd known him all their lives. Eden followed, not knowing whether to laugh or cry.

Chapter 19

A lone seagull soared on the warm air current high above the ocean, yet level with Eden where she stood on the cliff top. The breeze lifted her hair and hatless, it soon became free of its pins and blew about her head. Not that she cared. She was alone and it was late into the evening. She'd crept from the cottage and taken a walk along the cliff path to breathe in the fresh air and think.

She sniffed the salt air and paused to watch the waves tumbling on to the sand and rocks below. She'd been at the cottage for four weeks and with each day, she felt the heartache from the past slowly leave her. Coming here was as though she'd been given a new beginning. She still missed and mourned Nathan and Grandfather, but somehow the pain had lessened and the confusion and hurt were receding, too. Long walks along the beaches and country lanes around Whitby helped her to put her thoughts in order.

She wasn't the only one to benefit from this holiday. The girls had grown, they slept and ate well and used their energy up playing for hours in the sunshine on the beach with Charlie, who for once had colour in his face. Annabella and Carleton had also found the stay here valuable. They'd become closer, rediscovered their love, and spent time alone touring the countryside.

The cottage rang with the girls' laughter, Annabella's humming, Charlie's witty humour and Mellors's gentle conversation. Eden knew she was gradually healing, yet, despite the contentment she felt, there remained one nagging unease. Joel.

He was still in London and Eden missed him. She wanted him in her life permanently. They'd been given a second chance and she would grasp it this time. The only thing was to allow the girls a chance to know him better, as she needed to, before any decisions were made. However, at night her mind refused to sleep. Images of Joel's handsome face, his smile, or tender look kept her awake and yearning.

Out of the quiet the sound of panting reached her, breaking her out of her reverie. Coco, Charlie's cocker spaniel came bounding through the grass at her, his long ears flapping. She bent and patted him. 'Good boy.' Looking up, she smiled at Charlie, walking along the path.

'Care for some company?'

She waited until he was beside her and then linked her arm through his. 'I'm always happy to have you near.'

'The girls are fast asleep. They didn't even last to the end of the story.'

'Had they heard it before?' She grinned.

'Very funny.' He winked and gazed, out over the ocean, which shimmered gold as the setting sun was reflected on it. 'It will be hard to leave this place.'

'Yes.'

'I never expected to feel so at home here, but I do. Strange, isn't it?'

'If you are relaxed and content, then it's hard not to feel at home wherever you are.'

'I never experience that feeling from our house in London. I hate the city. So much noise and too many people.'

They walked on, comfortably silent until Charlie chuckled. 'You know, in the morning Mellors is rising at four to go fishing. One of the old fishermen told him it was the perfect time to go because the tides are right.'

'He's keen.'

Yes, and the more he catches, the more he wants to fish. But I am pleased for him. He doesn't have much time to himself. The break has done us all good.' He looked at her. 'Even you?'

'Yes, utterly. Just what I required.'

He placed his hand on her arm. 'Excellent. I hate seeing you unhappy.'

'Do you know what Joel said to me before we came here?'

'No, what?'

'That if I had a thought to remarry to think of him first.'

Charlie stopped. 'And did this surprise you?'

'Naturally it did.' She frowned. 'You don't seem surprised.'

'He's loved you for a long time, Eden. He stayed away as long as he did because he couldn't face coming home to see you married.'

'So, he truly loves me?'

'Absolutely. No question about it.'

'He told you this?' Could it be really true?

Charlie laughed and tweaked her nose, like he used to do when they were children. 'Of course, he told me.'

They walked along in silence as she digested his words. He loved her.... Her whole body seemed lighter at the thought.

Could she marry Joel? She loved him, of that there was no doubt, but could she move on with her life? Could she, after Nathan, be another's man's wife? But it wouldn't be just any man, it would be Joel. 'If I married Joel, I would be mistress of the Hall.'

'So?'

'From housekeeper to mistress.' She raised her eyebrows at him. 'Hardly acceptable to your friends, I would think.'

Shrugging, Charlie kicked at a small rock and watched it roll along the path. 'What few friends of mother and father's remain are not worth the worry. In fact, a lot of them think you are connected with the family anyway, you've been a part of us for so long. Besides, Joel has such a strong personality that people flock to him no matter what he does. You will simply be his wife, and it will be forgotten that you worked for us.'

'It will never be truly forgotten Charlie. People enjoy digging into other people's affairs. I would hate to bring scandal to the Bradbury name.'

'True, it's not always going to be easy. However, Joel thinks very little of narrow-minded people and rarely keeps their company.' He stopped and took her hands. 'I will tell you this, though, so you have all the facts before you decide one way or another. Joel won't stay in England all the time. He's mentioned plans of buying land in Africa and travelling. He's not content to stay beside his fireplace and read books for the rest of his life.'

She smiled. 'Yes, I know, he told me. He never could sit still for more than five minutes.'

Charlie tucked her hand back through his arm and they turned for home. 'I hope you do marry him, dearest. You both deserve to spend the rest of your lives together.'

'You are a romantic, Charles Bradbury.'

'Do you love him, Eden?'

'Yes, though I confess I'm scared.' She watched a boat on the horizon. 'For years I've tried to accept that Joel was lost to me. It's hard to imagine that the dream could come true at long last.'

He kissed her cheek. 'Then smile, my lovely. No more sadness.'

Tears welled. 'I want to smile, Charlie, really I do, but I feel as though there is this weight pressing on my chest. I can't get rid of it.'

'It'll take time. Too much has happened. Allow yourself to grieve.'

Yes.' She laid her head on his shoulder. 'What would I do without you?'

'Oh, that's easy, you'd be completely miserable for the rest of your life.' He laughed and tickled her in the ribs.

Grinning she pushed him away and then pulled him back again.

'What shall we do tomorrow, future sister-in-law?'

Determined to be more light-hearted from now on and to think positively, she laughed. 'Shall we go shopping? You can buy me something expensive.'

He spluttered. 'How expensive?'

'I'm not asking for diamonds.' Giggling like children, they entered the cottage.

~ ~ ~

The crush of the crowds filled the streets of Scarborough. Glorious weather of late summer and it be-

225

ing a Saturday, gave the people an excuse to swarm the streets and beaches of the coastal town.

Eden pushed her way through a throng of shoppers and out of the sweet shop. Thankful that, in the end the girls had stayed behind with Charlie, Eden purchased a bag of sweets for each of them. It would have been a nightmare keeping the girls close to her in this craziness. She, Annabella and Carleton left the cottage this morning for the shopping spree, with Charlie's list of things he wanted them to buy for him as well as themselves. Charlie, in his generous way, gave Eden a purse full of money and told her to have fun, while he and the girls would swim at the beach and search the rock pools. Hot and bothered as she mingled with the hordes, Eden wished she had stayed behind with them.

Standing on tiptoe, she scanned the street for any sign of Annabella, whose wide blue hat would be easy to spot.

'Eden.' Annabella rushed up from behind. 'Lord, it's so hot, and such a press of people.'

She looked up at the sky with its puffs of creamy cloud. 'This heat will likely bring a storm this afternoon.'

'Yes. We'll leave before then. Anyway, Carleton and I found a reputable hotel so I can have a bit of a rest. I've left him in the tearoom minding a table for us. Are you coming, or do you want to spend more time shopping?'

They moved closer to the building wall out of the way of pedestrians. 'No, I'll browse the shops. You two enjoy the time together. I might walk down to the sand or look around the markets.'

'Very well.' Annabella took a step, paused and then sighed. 'I should have left Carleton at the cottage

226

today so we could talk. We haven't discussed any-thing of importance since the holiday started.'

'It doesn't matter.' She smiled. 'I'm happy that you are spending the time with your husband.'

Annabella squeezed Eden's hand. 'We are getting along much better since we arrived at the cottage. I truly love him. We have talked and talked.'

'And the baby?' Eden moved aside for a large woman loaded down with parcels.

'The baby is his. I can feel it in my heart. To tell him anything else would cause too much pain and I would lose him.' She lifted her chin. 'I will not risk it.'

'And your living arrangements?'

Annabella glanced down at her light blue skirts and smoothed the matching jacket over her stomach. 'Carleton has agreed that we cannot go on as we are.'

'Understandable.'

'We have decided to...' She leaned in nearer. 'Our plans aren't finalized yet, but we have agreed to build a new house on the farm. His mother can live in her house and I'll have mine.'

Her tone darkened. 'My house will be grander than hers anyway and when she dies, hers will be knocked down.'

'Is it so terrible between you? Can you not tolerate her for Carleton's sake?'

'I do already,' Annabella scoffed. 'I've tried to be nice, but his mother believes I am all wrong for her precious Carleton and nothing will change her mind. Anyone else would have been happy that their son married well, but oh no, not her. She wanted him to marry a girl from another farm and annexe the two properties. She believes I am empty headed and vain and useless to Carleton. What does she know?'

Eden smiled. 'Indeed.'

'Oh, I know you laugh at me, Eden, but I'll show her. I can raise Carleton higher than she could ever have imagined. I won't settle for him wasting his time with cows and sheep.'

'What does Carleton want?'

Annabella smiled secretively, and the crowded street ceased to be there as they whispered. 'I know it's vulgar to talk of money, but he's managed to make a considerable sum of it from the new contacts he made on our honeymoon. He wants to enter politics. See what my influence has done?'

'So, you are both happy?'

'More than we have ever been.' Annabella beamed, bringing a new beauty to her face. 'Staying at the cottage was just what we needed. I'm glad we came, are you?'

Eden nodded. 'Very much so.'

'Good. Later, after we return to the cottage, shall we go for a walk and talk some more? I want you to tell me how you're feeling.

'I want to listen to you.'

'All right. I'd like that.'

'Lovely. Now I should go, or he'll think I've been spending money again. Shall we meet here, say, in two hours?' Annabella kissed her cheek and darted away. Eden smiled after her. Being pregnant didn't slow her dear friend down at all.

For a moment Eden hesitated, not knowing what to do or where to go next. The sun blistered the town, and suddenly thirsty, she decided to buy a drink and then find some shade. If she had the energy afterwards, she might walk up to the castle ruins. Wandering down the street, she gazed at the window displays, and entered a small book shop, where she purchased two of the books on Charlie's list.

Outside once more, she headed across the street. A wind had developed, and her skirts blew against her legs, hindering her progress. The change of weather had thinned the crowds, as the pillow clouds were replaced by grey smudges racing across the sky.

She abandoned the idea of walking to the castle ruins and ducked into a shop selling stationary. Lingering over the fine array of goods, she found a long, narrow cedar-wood case displaying two ink pens with golden nibs. Joel came to mind immediately, and she smiled at the shopkeeper as she bought them for him.

Leaving the shop, she couldn't wipe the smile from her face.

'Well I never!'

Eden, her parcels in one arm and her other hand holding on to her hat, turned to the woman who spoke. She frowned and then her eyes widened as she recognized Mrs Fleming standing at the entrance to a narrow alley. Of all the rotten luck!

Quickening her step, she paid no attention to the woman.

'Wait!' Fleming barged out into the street. 'Don't you ignore me, madam!'

Eden, her old hatred rising again, spun round to face her. 'I have nothing to say to you.'

'I have plenty to say to you.' Fleming marched up to Eden, her heavy brown skirt filthy, and the green shawl about her shoulders tatty.

'Go away, please.' Eden inched back.

'You're looking mighty fancy. Working your favours for Mister Charlie, are you? Or has he gone to his maker and left you a tidy sum for services rendered, hey?' Fleming sneered, her beady eyes dissecting the smart black clothes Eden wore and the parcels she held.

'You are disgusting.'

The wind whipped Fleming's greasy grey hair into her eyes, and she pushed it back with a dirt-ingrained hand. 'What are you doing here? Haunting me are you, like some living ghost?'

'Don't be ridiculous. I had no idea you lived here now.'

'No. How would you know anything?' Fleming leaned closer; her yellow teeth bared. 'Thanks to you, I have nothing. Did you know that?'

Eden smelt alcohol on the woman and straightened with disdain. You are solely responsible for your own predicament.'

'Horse shit!' Fleming shook her fist and people circled them warily. 'It's all your fault that I have no home, no job. Every time an employer wrote to dying Charlie-boy for a reference about me, he replied I wasn't trustworthy, but I bet you knew that, didn't you?'

'Actually, I knew of him doing it once, no more than that. Did you actually expect him to write a glowing character about you, after everything you did?'

'I expect to earn my living,' she spat.

'It had nothing to do with me.' Eden turned to go, but Fleming grabbed her arm.

'Everything that happened was your fault. So what are you going to do about it?'

'My fault?' Eden snorted. 'You believe that if it makes you feel better.'

Fleming ripped Eden's small velvet bag from her wrist and clutched it to her chest. 'This will do nice-ly.'

Instinct urged her to grab the bag back, but then she did a quick sum and realized the amount left in it was not worth the argument. The purse was a recent purchase and not sentimental to her. She shrugged. 'Have it. I don't care. You need it more than I do.'

'Well, yes I do, and you can always sell yourself to Mr Clifton.' Fleming grinned.

'I doubt he'd be interested, being dead.' At Fleming's shocked expression, Eden dipped her head in acknowledgement. 'Good day, Mrs Fleming.'

Ducking around the corner, Eden hurried up the next street and dashed into a lane behind a public house. Resting against a wall, she dosed her eyes, feeling stupid and slightly sick. Why did she have to run into that loathsome woman of all people?

Fleming couldn't hurt her now with her vicious tongue. Yet, why was she shaking? She looked at her trembling hands. Enough.

She'd had enough of the past affecting her.

Hitching the books into a better position, she took a deep breath and stepped out of the alley and into the street again. She wanted Joel and whatever future he offered. If that meant travelling, leaving England, then she would embrace it. She'd not live with ghosts riding her shoulders anymore.

Chapter 20

'Mam, come look at the tiny fish.' Lillie jumped about near a small rock pool.

'I'm coming.' Eden finished digging in the soft wet sand and gave the little spade to Josephine. 'Watch the tide. It's getting closer.' She smiled as small trickling waves rushed up to meet them, stopping only inches from the hole she and Josephine had dug.

'I'll dig a moat.' Josephine worked furiously, sand flying out behind her as she shovelled. 'Uncle Charlie said all castles need a moat.'

'Yes indeed.' Eden patted sand into a mound on top of the small hill they'd created. 'Castles have turrets, too.'

'And a drawbridge.'

Chuckling, Eden scooped up more sand. 'I don't fancy your chances of getting a drawbridge made, my love.'

A dog's bark echoed along the beach and they looked up as Mellors strode across the sand towards them, with Coco running ahead. Mellors waved.

Eden stood and dusted off her skirt. 'Not fishing?'

'No. I may have to return to the Hall tonight, so I've come down for a last look.' He stared out at the crashing waves.

'Why must you return?'

'Mister Charlie received a letter from the Hall, from Parkinson.'

'The Hall?' She frowned. 'Why would a letter from the steward cause alarm? Do they need you? Can Parkinson not cope?'

'Mister Joel has returned from London and is ill with a fever.'

Fever? Her hand flew up, as if to warm him from saying anything else that would hurt her. 'H-how ill is he?'

'We don't know for sure. Parkinson says he's been abed for three days.'

'I must go.' Her heart lodged in her throat, she glanced back at the girls. 'I need to speak with Charlie. Can you bring the girls up to the cottage?'

He nodded. 'Of course.'

Lifting her skirts, she ran as best she could on the sand and made her way up the cliff path to the cottage above. Joel ill. The words seemed emblazoned before her eyes. She could think of nothing else.

Out of breath, she scurried into the back of the cottage, not caring for the sand she scattered about the floor.

'Eden?' Charlie's call had her running into the front sitting room, which looked out over the ocean.

'Tell me what the letter said,' she wheezed, holding the stitch in her side.

'Calm down.' He smiled reassuringly and took her hand as she sat on the stool beside his chair. 'Parkinson says he arrived home three days ago and didn't feel well. He's been in bed ever since. The staff have been watching over him and the doctor has called once. Parkinson doesn't think it is serious but wanted to let me know.'

'He should never have gone to London alone.'

'Perhaps not, but you know how independent he is. Besides, he wanted us to have this holiday after all that happened.'

'He's alone, Charlie, and sick. Someone should be with him.'

'You, perhaps?' He gave her a wry smile. 'Go, dearest.'

'You won't come with me?'

He shook his head. 'No, Mellors and I will remain here with Annabella, Carleton and the girls.'

'The girls?' Her heart began a slow thud against her ribs.

'You trust us to care for them, don't you? And I doubt they wish to return just yet. But it is your choice.'

Time alone with Joel. Just her and Joel together. Tingles of expectation shivered her body at the thought.

'You've done nothing but pine for him, dearest. Go, Eden. Go and find the love waiting for you,' Charlie whispered.

She hugged him tightly. 'Thank you.'

'I expect news of an engagement on my arrival at the Hall.' He laughed.

Within the hour, she had washed and dressed and explained a hundred times to the girls why she was leaving them for a short time. With promises to write to them every day, they fully accepted that staying at the cottage would be far more fun than going back to the Hall.

As Annabella and the girls helped her pack, she grew nervous. What if Joel didn't want her there while he was sick?

What if his feelings had changed for her?

Finally, with nothing left to do, she kissed and hugged them all and climbed into the Bradbury carriage. Annabella stood near the window and clasped her hand. 'Don't hold back, Eden,' she whispered. 'It's time you were a Bradbury.' Her voice dropped even lower. 'And it's time the Bradbury nursery was in use again.' She winked and stepped back.

Eden laughed and waved as the carriage pulled away.

Annabella's quiet words sent a feverish heat to her cheeks, which felt hot to her touch. She closed her eyes and imagined Joel touching her, kissing her . . . She shook her head and sat up straighter. What nonsense. He was unwell and would likely sleep the whole time she was there.

By the time the carriage had travelled across half of Yorkshire and was drawing near to the Hall, Eden's confidence had dwindled, and her nervousness grown. Evening shadows stretched along the countryside. She yawned and flexed her neck and back. Her stomach was a tight knot and she shied away from thinking how Joel would react when he saw her.

Dusk was falling into night as the carriage trundled through the gates and up the drive. She glanced to her left in the direction of the woodland and smiled sadly. Although the cottage and her family had gone, it was still her home, the tall trees her protection.

A few lights twinkled in the Hall windows. She opened the carriage door and stepped down. A thousand thoughts went through her head. What if he had become worse? What if he didn't want her there? Some men hated being fussed over when they were sick.

The front door opened and one of the footmen, Dawson, came down the step. 'Mrs Harris? We had no word of your arrival.'

'No, it was a sudden decision. How is Master Bradbury?'

'Much better.' He smiled and puffed out his chest as though he was personally responsible for his recovery. 'He's out of bed and eating well.'

'Out of bed?' She hesitated, all thoughts of bedside nursing diminishing. Her nervousness grew making her shoulders tight with strain. Joel up and about and not needing her attentions? Instead, he would be the normal self-assured Joel, and one look from him would... No! She wouldn't think of how he made her feel. She needed time to compose herself. The woodland drew her gaze. 'Dawson can you see to my luggage? I need to stretch my legs.'

'Certainly, Mrs Harris.'

Lifting her skirt, she hurried around the side of the house and across the gardens. The closer she came to the woodland the faster she went. Her brisk walk slowed when she entered the shadows of the trees. A bird called. Weaving through the trees, she lightly touched each trunk. The damp smell of vegetation filled her nose, a scent as familiar to her as her own name.

She looked up at the canopy and smiled at the rising moon shimmering on the leaves. The tension left her body and she breathed in deeply. An owl hooted, filling the quiet. A scuffle came from beneath the bracken to her right and she glimpsed the white of a rabbit's tail. The darkness didn't bother her. The monsters of the flesh always frightened her more than noises of the wood.

Eventually, she came to the ruins of the cottage. For a while she stood and remembered the people who once lived there, her parents and grandparents, Nathan, the ones who had loved her. Then her thoughts drifted to the future. What would the rest of her life be like?

'Eden.'

She turned and smiled at Joel, not at all surprised he had found her. She held out her hand and he came to her and took it.

'What are you doing?'

'I was revisiting the past.'

'And the future?' He gazed at the charred timber.

'Ah, it will take care of itself I think.' He seemed far from being ill, thinner perhaps, but thankfully not on death's doorstep.

'This will always be your home, won't it?' He turned and stared at her. 'Could you ever leave it?'

'This woodland is my home because I was never unhappy here, despite what Clifton did to me over there.' She waved towards the left in the direction of the spot she'd never visited since that day. 'Despite that I never hated the woodland. How could I? So many times, I sensed Clifton watching me at the Hall or in the gardens, but here, I was safe. Here I could escape into the trees and he could never find me.'

His hand tightened around hers. 'Then how did he that day?'

'Because I left the path to go mushroom picking. There were a great patch of them on the west side, just inside the tree line. He saw me as he rode past, but I didn't see him. He was upon me before I had a chance to run.' Her hands twitched her skirt. 'I've never eaten mushrooms since.'

He nodded, his throat working. 'Had he not hanged himself, had he got free somehow, I would have seen him suffer. In fact, I think I would have-'

'Don't, Joel. It's done. Finished.'

They remained silent for a while before he looked at her. 'Have you thought about my offer?'

'Which one?'

'Both.'

'Yes.'

He sucked in a lungful of air. 'The others remained in Whitby?'

'Yes.' She wondered at his change of topic, the steering of it to a safer ground. Joel must have been as frightened as her about confirming his feelings. 'Parkinson sent Charlie a letter. I came to tend to you and the house while you were sick.'

'I was under the weather when I returned from London, a mere chest cold, that's all.'

'And being out here in the night air isn't good for you either. But, thank God it was nothing worse, we were all so worried.'

'Did you worry?'

She frowned at him, the darkness hiding his expression.

'What kind of question is that?'

'A sensible one. The kind a man asks when he's not sure what the response will be.'

'You aren't asking me whether I'm worrying about your health, are you?'

'It's becoming cold, let's return to the house.'

Silently, they walked back through the wood, across the field and into the gardens. Eden's mind whirled with questions and thoughts, but she said nothing.

In the drawing-room, a fire blazed and she went to hold her hands out to it though she wasn't cold.

Joel added another log to the fire. 'I'm sorry Parkinson troubled you all. He should have kept his own counsel.'

'He thought he was doing the right thing, and he did. What if you had been dreadfully ill? We had to know.'

'Yes, all right. I see your point.' He smiled the blue of his eyes softening to violet in the lamp light. 'I had plans of travelling to Whitby, but I was a bit low after the operation and then the cold in my chest didn't help.'

She glanced at his arm, hanging free by his side, and realized the sling had gone. 'Was the operation a success?'

'Yes.' He rubbed his shoulder. 'I can't use the arm too much until the wound has healed properly, but I should get full movement within a few months.'

'I'm glad. Does it hurt?'

'A little.'

'Shouldn't you be wearing your sling?'

He grinned. 'Yes, but it annoys me. I hate being restricted.'

'You always did.' She glanced to the fire, watching the dancing flames. Every nerve ending seemed to be on alert, she needed to sit down.

'Are you hungry?'

Managing a smile, she nodded. Food was the last thing she wanted, but they'd have to do something. She suddenly felt awkward and unprepared. Instead of tending to a sick man, she had to deal with the two of them alone in the house. Chancing a look at him, she found his gaze on her.

'Don't stare at me like that, my love,' he murmured deep in his throat. 'I'm as nervous as you. I feel like an uncouth boy of eighteen at this moment.'

She closed her eyes, aching for him to hold her. The way he looked at her set her trembling like a young girl. Only, her body wasn't that of a young girl, it was waking up, and yearning for the physical completion between two people.

'Eden...'

Her eyes flew open and he was inches from her, a hot look in his eyes.

'Sweetheart.' He lowered his head and his lips lightly touched hers. 'It feels like I've been waiting all my life to hold you,' he whispered against her mouth.

Quivers of delight shimmered along her body and she strained for more of his touch.

'Joel,' she sobbed. Unable to hold back another second, she drew his head down for a crushing kiss that left him in no doubt what she wanted.

Joel pressed her to him, bending her against his body. 'Christ, I love you.' He rained kisses over her face. 'Say you love me, I beg you.'

'I do, my darling, I do. I always have.' Their tears mingled.

She kissed away his sorrow of years lost. 'Don't ever leave me again.'

He held her tighter. 'I won't, I promise. You're mine.'

'I have been yours all my life.' She cupped his face and smiled into his eyes.

'You will marry me?' He kissed her softly, reverently.

'Yes.' Her heart sighed, once more whole.

Joel kissed her again and then drew her down on to the sofa. 'I have plans, but we can-'

She placed a finger to his lips. 'Tell me about it later, my love.'

Wrapping her arms about his neck, she nibbled his ear and the skin under his jaw. She adored the freedom of finally being able to caress him. Desire curled within her body.

'Tell me your thoughts.' His hands roamed over her body, as if to familiarize himself with her.

'They are all jumbled up, making no sense.'

'Mine too, but one thing is clear. I love you and want you beside me for the rest of my life.'

Rubbing her nose against his, she grinned. 'Annabella said the nursery needs to be in use again and I agree.'

He frowned. It took a moment for her words to impact on him and she laughed when he caught on to her thinking. A slow smile lit up his face and she took a deep breath at the magnificence of him.

'I think my sister is right for once.' He brought her hand up and placed his lips to each finger. 'I would like a houseful of children.'

'Steady on. One or two is quite sufficient.' She grinned and stood, pulling him up with her. 'Perhaps you should take me upstairs so we can practise.'

Joel laughed and then drew her to him, suddenly serious again. 'We'll be happy, Eden I promise. I'll take care of you and the girls. I will treat them as though they are mine.'

She played with one of the shiny brass buttons on his uniform. 'If you can love them, Joel then they will be.'

'I love them already, for they are a part of you. Every time I look at them, I see you as a girl. The little girl who stole my heart.'

His words melted her heart, but she still worried. 'Does it matter that I'm not of your class?'

He drew back, his eyes narrowing. You need to ask that question of me?'

'Yes, for it isn't going to be easy. Your father didn't want you marrying me, maybe-'

'My father made many mistakes. He wanted the best for me, I know that, but he didn't understand that no other woman could outshine you.'

'Your friends expect-'

He silenced her with a kiss. 'My friends will only remain as such if they accept you. I can live without them, but not without you.'

She sighed against him, closing her eyes as his arms encircled her and held her close. She felt his heart thumping beneath her cheek and breathed in his slight cologne. No matter where she lived, in Bradbury Hall, her woodland, or some foreign country, as long as she was in Joel's arms, she was home.

About the Author

Award winning & Amazon UK Bestseller Anne-Marie Brear has been a life-long reader and started writing in 1997 when her children were small. She has a love of history, of grand old English houses and a fascination of what might have happened beyond their walls. Her interests include reading, travelling, watching movies, spending time with family and eating chocolate - not always in that order! She is the author of historical family saga novels.

If you enjoyed my story please leave a review online, it helps an author very much, and we appreciate them more than you know.

Thank you
AnneMarie Brear
http://www.annemariebrear.com
Facebook: /annemariebrearauthor
Twitter: https://twitter.com/annemariebrear

Eden's Conflict

Lightning Source UK Ltd.
Milton Keynes UK
UKHW010002081021
391837UK00002B/699

9 781999 865023